Jingle Blades

A SWEET CHRISTMAS ROMANTIC COMEDY

THE PEPPERMINT PLAYBOOK
BOOK ONE

TOMI TABB

Paperback ISBN: 978-1-969184253

eBook ISBN: 978-1-969184246

First edition

First published by Pas de Chat Publications 2025 Copyright © 2025 by Tomi Tabb

 Formatted with Vellum

Chapter One

CHLOE

The dense forest of pine trees thins, giving way to a cluster of chalet-style buildings with turrets and steeply pitched roofs. Their facades are a warm blend of sandstone, cream stucco, and dark hand-carved wood. Wrought-iron balconies curve along the upper floors, wrapped in evergreen garlands and twinkling lights, reminding everyone that Christmas is only a week away.

Then I see it—the rink. My breath catches. The smooth frozen surface reflects the lights strung overhead and the snow-dusted mountain peaks beyond. For a second, all I can think is *this* is where I get to skate this week. Not in a dim practice arena or under flickering fluorescents, but here, in this storybook setting.

"*This* is the Mynt Peak Resort?" I ask, my nose pressed against the window. "It looks like something straight out of a European postcard."

"Yes, Miss Reynolds." The driver chuckles. "Where do you think Mr. Mynt took his inspiration from?"

"We're in the big leagues now," I whisper to myself, pinching my forearm, still unable to believe how far I've climbed up in the world since winning the US national figure skating title earlier this year. I may come from a wealthy family, but I've been financially independent since I was eighteen. And on my own longer than that. Staying in a place like this is a dream.

Less than six months ago, whenever I traveled for a competition, I was googling motels under a hundred dollars a night and praying the bathroom had halfway decent water pressure, and the walls weren't paper-thin. And now? Now I'm staying at a five-star resort where the fireplace in the lobby is larger than the bathroom in my apartment.

As the car pulls up to the front entrance, a doorman in a forest-green pressed coat opens the door, and the resort's valet team rushes forward to unload my luggage. They're like a well-oiled Formula One pit crew.

"Chloe! Chloe!" a familiar voice shouts.

I turn just in time to see a blond pixie come flying past the doorman. Emma barrels into me with one of her signature bear hugs, knocking me back a step against the SUV.

"Oof. It's good to see you too." We both start laughing. Some things never change. Emma's always been tiny but mighty.

Standing a hair under five feet tall, Emma always wears her strawberry-blond hair piled high in a bun and has ice-blue eyes. She's as close to the real-life Tinker Bell as you can get. Like me, she's twenty-three years old. We met in California when we were freshmen at Fresno State, and have been best friends ever since.

"Why didn't you text me that you were almost here? I had to hear the valet guys announce your name over the radio," she says, finally letting go of me.

"Cut me some slack. I didn't even know where we *were*." I laugh. "I've only been to Winterbrook one other time. After we left the Denver airport, it was just pine trees and snow for miles. I could've sworn we were driving in circles."

Emma smirks. "Okay, fine. Being lost in the forest is a valid excuse." She glances at her watch, then bites her lip. "Hmm . . . technically, it's a little early for me to clock out for my lunch break, but since you're here . . ."

Her voice trails off. Her eyes gleam the same way they used to when we'd go on our midnight milkshake runs.

I snort. "Didn't your shift start at ten? You haven't even been on the clock for an hour yet. It's only ten fifty-five. Won't your boss get mad?"

"He's not here yet," Emma says with a shrug. "I've got the opening shift at the concierge desk today, which basically means all I have to do is smile at people, hand out resort maps, and pretend to look busy until noon."

"Emma." I groan and face-palm. "What if somebody actually *needs* you?"

"I put the 'We'll Be Back Soon' sign up," she says with an air of confidence. "Besides, I'm with *you*. You're a VIP guest." She rests a hand on my shoulder. "Mr. Mynt gave the resort staff strict orders. All the athletes coming here for the Mynt to Make a Difference charity event this week are to be treated like royalty. I'm just doing what he wants."

Barry Mynt is the eccentric owner of Mynt Athletic Clothing and the resort. He likes to name things after himself. I've only met the man once, but he's not the type of person you're likely to forget. He may be in his early sixties, but his energy and enthusiasm would make you think he's still in his twenties.

I sigh. As much as I'd love nothing more than to catch up with Emma, preferably over mugs of hot chocolate by the fireplace, I don't want my bestie to lose her job. I know how hard she's worked to earn one of the resort's coveted concierge positions.

"Em, seriously," I say, lowering my voice. "I'll be here for five whole days. We've got plenty of time to catch up."

She gives me a look, the kind that says, *You're being reasonable, and I don't like it.* "Fine. But only because I know where your suite is and I can ambush you later." We enter the lobby. "At least let me help you get checked in."

We enter the lobby. Soaring timber beams stretch overhead. A massive stone fireplace anchors the far wall, its hearth framed by cozy armchairs and oversized plaid pillows.

"It smells so good in here," I say, pausing just inside the doorway. "Like fresh pine and . . ." I frown, trying to place the warm, spiced note dancing under my nose. I inhale again, slower this time. "Something like . . . cinnamon?"

"Mulled wine?" Emma offers.

I sniff the air again. "Yeah, that's it. Mulled wine."

Emma grins. "I'll let you in on a trade secret. There are diffusers spread throughout the lobby that pipe the scent inside. Mr. Mynt had it created exclusively for the holidays here at the resort."

"I'm impressed," I murmur, my gaze sweeping across the room.

"It's all about the details. That's why we're a five-star resort."

She's right. The details are everywhere. Garlands of cedar and twinkle lights wrap around every column, dotted with velvet bows and sprigs of holly. A pair of reindeer sculptures made entirely of silver bells flank the grand staircase. In the center of the lobby, a towering Christmas tree sparkles with vintage-style bulbs. And near the check-in desk, there's even a life-sized gingerbread cabin.

"Is that real?" I ask, pointing to the gingerbread house.

"What do you think?" Emma asks.

I squint at it. "It is, isn't it?"

"Ding, ding, ding. Ten points to Chloe Reynolds." But before I can wander over for a closer look, Emma steers me gently toward the front desk. "Come on, gingerbread later. Let's get you checked in."

A few hours later, once Emma's *officially* on her lunch break and no longer sneaking around like a criminal, we head to the resort's café just off the lobby. Inside, it's warm and bustling, with floor-to-ceiling windows that overlook the snowy courtyard and rink. The air smells like espresso and freshly baked bread. We grab a table in the back corner.

"So what's it like being the best figure skater in the country?" Emma asks, taking a bite of her sandwich and eyeing me like she already knows I'll downplay it.

My cheeks burn. "The same as being the fifth best. Just with a little more funding."

She rolls her eyes. "Chloe. You seriously still think your win was a fluke?"

I stay silent and lean back in my chair, letting my gaze drift to the snowflakes falling outside. Nationals is the most important domestic competition for American figure skaters. It's the one that decides who goes to Worlds, and in Olympic years, who gets to represent the red, white, and blue on the biggest stage of all.

Normally, everyone brings their A-game. But this year? It was a total splat-fest. Falls, under-rotations, missed elements—you name it, it happened. It was as if the ice was cursed.

Everyone had a horrible competition. Except for me. That night, I was one of the few people who skated clean. I've never been one of the skaters with the most technically difficult program, and usually, that holds me back. But this time, it worked in my favor.

"I won because everyone else messed up," I say in a low voice.

Emma shakes her head. "No, Chloe. You're looking at it backward. You were calm and cool, and delivered when it mattered. That's not luck. That's what champions do. And if it was really a fluke, you wouldn't have been the top American finisher at Worlds."

I stir my soup, watching the steam rise, not quite ready to meet her eyes. I guess she has a point. Worlds was strange too. Even though it was my first time, I felt like there was no pressure. The American Skating Union just wanted me to finish high enough to ensure the US earned a full three spots for the Olympic Games. As long as I skated like I do every day in practice, I knew it was within reach.

But I did better than that. I skated the best programs of my life and finished fourth. Amaya Gilcrest and Samantha Porter, both previous national champs, were expected to challenge for the podium and finish ahead of me. I was supposedly the weak link.

But once again, like Nationals, they both fell apart in the free skate, and suddenly, I was the top American. Sure, a medal would've been nice. But honestly? I'm just happy I can officially call myself the fourth-best skater in the world.

I take another sip of soup, letting the warmth settle in my chest. Then I change the subject. "How's your family?"

Emma's parents own the local florist shop, the one that

supplies all the flowers, gift baskets, and a few other special amenities for the resort.

"They're good. Mom and Dad would love to have you over for dinner at least once while you're here."

"I'd love to see them," I reply with a smile. "And, um, how's your brother?"

"Drew's good." She shrugs, and frustratingly, doesn't offer any more information.

I try not to look too disappointed, but I was hoping for at least *some* news. Even a tiny breadcrumb. Drew is four years older than Emma, and he's always had a way of causing my heart to play hopscotch whenever we've crossed paths.

Drew's the kind of guy you don't forget easily. He's tall, broad-shouldered, and built like someone who runs marathons for fun—which he does. His wavy nutmeg-colored hair somehow always looks perfectly tousled, even after running ten miles.

His eyes are a warm-brown, like maple syrup in sunlight. But my favorite feature is his grin. It's a smug, smoldering kind of grin, like Flynn Rider from *Tangled*. Personality wise, Drew thinks he's funny—and unfortunately, he is.

"Is he, um, still doing marketing for Pacific Skyways?" I ask, trying to sound casual as I take a sip of my soup.

"Nope. They filed for bankruptcy and laid off his whole department." Emma makes a face. "I could've sworn I told you that."

"Nuh-uh." I shake my head. "When did that happen?"

"About six months ago. He's moved back in with Mom and Dad and is working in the shop part-time until he figures out what he wants to do next."

"And you're just mentioning it now?"

She shrugs. "It didn't seem all that important."

Maybe I'll actually get to see him. My stomach performs the type of somersaults that would earn bonus points from any Olympic judge. He's never looked at me as more than his little sister's friend. But Christmas *is* around the corner, and who knows . . . if I find a little mistletoe, maybe I'll be lucky enough to steal a kiss.

Chapter Two

DREW

The last thing I expected this morning was to be knee-deep in snow, hauling arrangements of poinsettias, amaryllises, and paperwhites from my parents' shop into the Mynt Peak Resort. But here we are.

"This is the last one," I say, slightly out of breath as I set the planter down near the front tables.

Christine, one of the catering and convention services managers, gives the setup a once-over. "What about the boughs of holly?"

"They'll be here tomorrow morning," I tell her. "Mom's still spraying them with sealant, so they don't dry out before we get them up." I pass her the clipboard for a sign-off.

"Perfect. We can always count on your parents to come through for us. Mr. and Mrs. Mynt will be thrilled when they see everything." She scribbles her name on the form. "Your parents must be so excited to have you back home. Especially this time of year to help with all the extra deliveries."

"They are," I say half-heartedly. "Well, I'll, uh, see you

tomorrow." I collect the clipboard and power walk outside, letting out a deep breath.

Being back in Winterbrook was never part of the plan. When I opened that email from Pacific Skyways informing me that I'd been laid off, it felt like I was stepping into the Twilight Zone. Just like that, all the late nights and promotions I'd been chasing were for nothing. I'd have to start my career again from scratch.

I spent two months applying to every marketing job I could find that would keep me in the LA area. All that happened was I burned through most of my savings and only landed a couple interviews. I realized pretty fast that Plan A wasn't panning out. So I went to Plan B and came home. I told myself it would be temporary—a few weeks, max. That was six months ago. And now here I am, still working in my parents' flower shop as the delivery guy.

It's not the work that bothers me. It's the giant question mark hanging over my head about my future. Some days, I feel like I'm stuck in a life that doesn't fit anymore—like I'm wearing someone else's clothes and hoping no one notices.

And as much as I try to laugh it off, there's this voice inside my head that keeps asking What if this is it? What if I already peaked and being the delivery guy is the best I can do?

The truth is, I'm over the corporate grind. I've had enough of the endless meetings that could've been emails and spending eight hours a day in a tiny cubicle, quietly losing my mind over searching for new buzzwords.

I want something different. Something that doesn't make me dread Mondays. I don't have it all figured out yet, but I've started kicking around a few ideas. I know I want to do something that's more hands-on and allows me to be more creative. It's why I originally got into marketing in the first place.

But for now, the future will have to wait. I still have a van half-full of fir trees and holiday arrangements to deliver. I head down the long hallway toward the lobby. There are oversized wreaths, garlands twinkling with white lights, and a tree that's large enough to sit in New York's Rockefeller Plaza. I weave around it, pass the roaring fireplace, and make my way to the concierge desk.

My sister is alone. Perfect. "You know, you could at least *pretend* to be working." I stroll up to her and peer over the edge. Emma's hunched over the open top drawer like she's one of Notre Dame's famous gargoyles. "You do realize it's obvious to anyone with eyes that you're on your phone, right? Aren't you breaking concierge rule number one of what *not* to do?"

Emma barely glances up. "It's just for a second. The tickets for that concert Mom and Dad mentioned last month drop at three, and I didn't want to miss getting into the virtual queue."

I raise a brow. "What band? The Midnight Peppers?"

That's the only group I can think of. Our parents have been following the Peppers since they were our age. Whenever we'd go anywhere in the car as kids, we'd have to fight our parents for the CD player. Spoiler alert, they always won. Dad even has this tour shirt from the seventies that's so worn and thin, I have no idea how it's still being held together.

"Uh-huh. And this tour is special. Neil, the original drummer, is back for a limited number of stops, including Denver. So every Peppers fan in the area is gonna wanna go."

Dang it. Why didn't I think of getting them tickets?

Emma's gonna be the favorite child if she pulls this off. "They won't sell out that quickly," I say, trying to downplay it.

"Says you." Her fingers fly across the screen. "There. I'm in. And there's still"—she pauses, then squints at the screen—"three hundred and ten people ahead of me. Fingers crossed it doesn't sell out before I get to the checkout."

My eyes widen. "Seriously?"

"Uh-huh." She waves the phone in front of me.

"If I give you some money, any chance the tickets can be from *both* of us for Christmas?"

"That depends." She snorts. "How much are you willing to throw in?"

I dry swallow. Expensive gifts aren't exactly in my budget right now. But I can't be outdone by my little sister. And it *is* for our parents. And I really don't feel like going to the mall. I haven't done any of my gift shopping yet. "Two hundred?"

"Deal."

We shake on it. I'll need to put in some extra hours at the shop this week to cover it. The place might be a family business, but I'm still only making minimum wage.

"Are you heading home?" Emma asks.

"I've got two more deliveries to make first. But after that, I am. I've been up since four-thirty, and I'm ready for a nap." I can't wait until I have a job with normal hours again. I'm done with the pre-dawn flower-shipment nonsense.

"Well before you take off, can you check on the aquarium near the gift shop? A guest said one of the fish was looking 'suspiciously floaty' and there was a lot of green stuff on the glass?"

"Suspiciously floaty? Green stuff?" I echo, frowning. "That sounds like code for 'already gone to the great fishbowl in the sky' and an algae bloom. Who normally takes care of the tank?"

"No idea. I texted the boss, but he hasn't gotten back to me yet." She shrugs. "Anyway, you're the resident fish expert. I figured you could take a look. The sooner it's fixed, the better," she says, already waving me off as a guest approaches. "Might as well put your skills to good use, Aquaman."

"Fine," I mutter, heading toward the hallway.

I shouldn't be the one doing this. Hotel aquariums aren't in my job description. But I can't help myself, and Emma knows it. I've always loved aquariums and have kept them since I was a kid as a hobby. There's something about the calm, the colors, the slow drift of fish through water that gets me every time.

From a distance, the fifty-gallon tank looks like a toddler went wild with green finger paint. Three of the aquarium's four glass panels are coated in a thick layer of algae. Up close, it's just as bad. The decorative rocks are fuzzy with green, and the water has a cloudy tint that practically screams neglected filters. A few fish hover near the bottom, clearly miserable.

I crouch down. This doesn't look like one of those setups with a hidden filtration system in a back room. I press along the cabinet until I find the latch for the access panel. When it pops open, I'm greeted by gunky tubing, a pump that sounds like it's on its last leg, and water that's too warm.

I frown. Whoever was supposed to be maintaining this thing should be fired. Judging by the state of it, I'd bet the tank hasn't been touched in two or three months. I can't just walk away from this. Not when it's this bad.

I roll up my sleeves and grab the algae scraper and the siphon. At least they left the basic cleaning tools behind. As I work, muscle memory takes over—scrape, siphon, scrape, siphon. Bit by bit, the tank starts to look less like a science experiment and more like something a fish might actually want to live in.

As weird as it may seem, there's something calming about cleaning the tank. Some of the tension leaves my body, but I'm still angry. These fish deserve better. And I'm going to make sure the hotel's manager or whoever is in charge hears about this.

I set the algae-filled bucket on the ground beside me and reach for the siphon hose, planning to dump the water and clean up my mess before I find one of the resort's higher-ups. I kneel down. The bucket is heavy, but nothing I can't handle.

As I straighten my legs and lift the bucket to my chest, someone comes barreling around the corner at full speed and slams straight into me. I stagger backward, and a tidal wave of grimy greenish water splashes up over my arms, chest, and face. It's slimy, and stinks like, well, fish.

Chapter Three

CHLOE

Why did I have to hit Snooze on my phone?! I'm supposed to be at the Mynt to Make a Difference charity orientation in less than ten minutes. I can't be late. Not on day one!

I power walk down the hallway and round the corner at full speed, glancing at my watch.

In that split second, I slam into something—or rather, someone. There's a muffled grunt, followed by a huge splash.

I stumble back, blinking in horror. The sleeves of my pearly-white sweater are soaked. And covered in . . . green sludge? Ugh. I take another step back and land in a puddle of water. It goes through my white Keds. Great. Just great.

Then I see him. A guy sitting on the ground, shaking water off his arms. I gulp. He's taken the direct hit. His blue polo shirt and brown cargo pants are plastered in the green slime. It's on his arms, his face, even dripping from his hair.

Guilt floods my system. "Oh my gosh, I'm so sorry!" I sputter. "Are you okay?"

He turns to me, pushing soggy strands of hair out of his eyes, and glares. "I'm fine. No thanks to you," he mutters.

I inhale sharply. It's as if somebody has dropped me in the middle of the Arctic Ocean and I've turned into an ice cube. Of all the people I could've crash into, it would be Drew Sullivan. The universe hates me.

I swallow hard. He hasn't changed at all. He still has the same strong jawline and wavy nutmeg-colored hair. Despite the green muck, he's still incredibly attractive.

My heart skips a beat. And not in the romantic, butterflies-and-stolen-glances kind of way. More like the I-need-to-get-out-of-here-as-fast-as-humanly-possible kind of way.

He blinks through the mess, trying to assess the damage. "You try to do something nice, and this is the thanks you get," he grunts, reaching for a roll of paper towels. "It's the last time I help Emma out."

I tug my hair forward like a curtain and duck my head, praying he won't recognize me right now. "I'm so, so, so sorry. I didn't see you."

"No kidding," he says without looking at me.

"Is there anything I can do to help?"

"No."

Ouch. I wince, hugging my soggy arms to my chest. This is *not* how I pictured our reunion going. And as much as I want to crawl into the nearest potted plant and disappear, I have to get to that orientation. I was already running late before I turned Drew Sullivan into an unwilling aquarium exhibit. "I hate to do this to you, but I have to run. There's this meeting I—"

"I got that . . ." He trails off, finally looking at me. His eyes narrow. A glint of recognition flickers behind them. "Wait a second," he says slowly. "Chloe, is that you?"

My stomach drops. "Um . . . hi," I stammer.

And there it is. He *does* remember me. All at once, I'm equal parts horrified and giddy? I mean, this isn't exactly how I imagined Drew recognizing me, but still, he knows who I am.

Luckily, before he can say anything else, a woman shouts my name. "Miss Reynolds! There you are!" The woman, who is in a fuchsia blazer and wearing a lanyard, comes hurrying over, holding a clipboard like it's a weapon of efficiency. "I've been looking for you. All the other athletes have checked in and we're just about to start."

"I'm coming," I say quickly, grateful for the lifeline. "I just had a little . . . accident."

"I can see that," she says, her eyes flicking over the scummy pond we've managed to create. "Should I even ask, Drew?"

"No," he says flatly.

She sighs and shakes her head. "I'll have someone from housekeeping come help you. As for you, Miss Reynolds . . . We need to get going."

The event coordinator turns and walks briskly down the hallway. I shoot Drew one last awkward grimace, then scramble after her.

As we round the corner, I chance another glance over my shoulder. He's cleaning his arms with paper towels. He lifts his chin. Our eyes lock. For several seconds, he watches me. My pulse races, and for a moment, I can't breathe.

His face softens. The frustration from earlier slips away as one corner of his mouth lifts in the smallest of smiles. Heat rushes to my cheeks. I have to get out of here. Swallowing hard, I dart inside the safety of the ballroom.

Chapter Four

DREW

I stand in the middle of the hallway my thoughts racing faster than a team of sled dogs trying to win the Iditarod.

Chloe Reynolds. I haven't seen her in a few years. I wish I'd gotten to speak to her more before she ran away. I could've asked her how she's been. Or how she's enjoying being in Winterbrook. But it was like my body was made of wood. I couldn't get my mouth to utter a single word. I rake a hand through my damp hair and glance down at my soggy shoes. Smooth, Sullivan.

Just as I'm trying to figure out how I'm gonna see her again, a member of the hotel housekeeping team rounds the corner, pushing a cart stacked high with towels and a bright yellow "Caution: Wet Floor" sign. She takes one look at the puddle, then at me, and lets out a long sigh.

I wince, feeling guilty, even though it wasn't my fault. "I'm sorry," I say.

Behind her is the front desk manager. His face is filled with tight lines. "Mr. Sullivan," he says, folding his hands in front of him. "I heard we have a situation." His eyes travel to the puddle on the carpet, then to the half-empty aquarium, and finally to me. "What happened?"

"Minor flooding," I mutter, gesturing toward the mess. "But don't worry. There weren't any fatalities."

"I see." He exhales slowly, and some of the tension leaves his shoulders. "And is there a particular reason *you* were handling the fish tank?"

I nod toward the aquarium, water still dribbling from one edge. "Because whoever the hotel hired to take care of it hasn't been doing their job."

His brows lift a fraction of an inch.

"The tank was clogged, filthy, and the fish were barely holding on. You could see the algae buildup from across the hall. I wasn't trying to redecorate your lobby; I was just trying to help the fish survive until a new aquarium company could be called in."

I leave out the part about Emma asking me for help. I'm a nice older brother. I want her to keep her job. She doesn't need to get pulled into this. But I do add, "It's the kind of thing that you don't want your guests to notice. Especially for a five-star luxury resort that's at capacity for the holidays."

Those words have the intended effect. The manager stands taller. "And you're an expert?"

"Not exactly," I say. "But I've been keeping fish tanks since I was a kid."

He strokes his jaw. "Well, I know your family has a long history of working with the resort and that gives you certain liberties. But in the future, I'd appreciate it if you could alert the staff before attempting any more aquarium triage."

"Yes, sir."

He sighs and gazes at the tank. "It's the week before

Christmas. I doubt we're going to be able to get anyone in to service this thing before the new year."

"I could look after it. Just for a week or two." My offer surprises both of us. I already have a long list of responsibilities to do for my parents, and now I'm adding this to it.

His brows lift slightly. "You want the job?"

"I guess so."

The manager gives me a slow nod. "If you're certain, I'll have HR draw up a temporary contract. Liability and all that."

"Of course," I say. We shake hands just as Emma appears at the end of the hallway, looking like she's just finished running a marathon. She skids to a stop, eyes widening at the sight of the mess.

"Drew—"

"Everything's fine," I say quickly, cutting her off. "Mr. Langston and I have it all worked out."

I give her a look that I hope translates to *Please don't say you asked me to touch the tank.*

"Well, if that's all, I'll notify HR and have them contact you about the details. Go ahead and do what you need to do with *that*." He nods toward the tank. Turning to the housekeeper, he adds, "Let's get this cleaned up before one of our guests ends up in the ER."

"Yes, sir," she replies, already moving toward the puddle.

Langston glances between me and Emma, then checks his watch. "I have a meeting, but if you need anything else, your sister knows how to get in touch with me."

With that, he strides off, shoes squelching faintly.

Emma waits until he's out of earshot before whispering, "I'm so, so sorry. Please tell me you didn't just volunteer to clean fish poop all week."

"Technically, I volunteered to keep the fish alive. The poop's just part of the package."

She groans. "I owe you. Big time."

"You do." And not just for the aquarium. I could've thrown her under the bus back there, but I didn't. Older-brother points, earned.

"Can I buy you lunch to make up for it?"

"Sure," I say. "I need a new set of clothes too."

"Deal." She nods. "I'll meet you at the café in about an hour."

"Sounds good." I turn back to the tank, watching the tetra fish dart through the freshly filtered water, and try not to think too hard about my sister's best friend.

Chapter Five

CHLOE

"**H**ere we are. Feel free to sit anywhere you'd like," the coordinator says, ushering me in with a brisk wave.

"Thanks," I whisper.

Scanning the room, I avoid eye contact with as many people as I can and gravitate to a seat in the back half of the room and exhale. Everyone here is a professional athlete who works with the Mynt Athletic Clothing company.

I recognize a few of the faces. There's the football player Ledger Bishop. Tennis player Eddie Evans. And snowboarder Aspen Sterling. All big-time names!

The others are less familiar, but they all give off an aura of confidence that makes me believe they're all huge successes in their respective fields. Like the guy sitting four rows away from me, also by himself. He has brown hair, gray eyes, and a short, trimmed beard. With those broad, muscular shoulders, I bet he plays a sport like hockey.

I fan myself and sink lower into my seat. I can't believe I'm sitting in the same room as all of them. They all look so put together in their crisp button-down shirts, designer jackets, and high-end jewelry. And here I am wearing a stained sweater, shoes, and jeans.

My cheeks burn. It's my first major event with Mynt Athletic Clothing, and I should've known the dress code was going to be business casual. I wish I would've gotten the memo to dress nicer. But it's too late now. I roll up the sleeves of my sweater, hoping to hide the worst of the stains.

"Welcome, everyone!" a woman with short curly blond hair says as she enters the stage. "We're thrilled to have you all here to support an incredible cause, Mynt to Make a Difference." She says a few more words, then introduces the owner and CEO, Barry Mynt.

True to his larger-than-life personality, he's dressed in a hunter-green suit covered in tiny peppermints. It works well with his white hair and neat beard. I shouldn't be surprised, given that every time I've seen him, his clothing has had a mint theme to it. I'm half-surprised he doesn't have a candy company that specializes in mint chocolates in his portfolio.

Taking hold of the mic, Mr. Mynt smiles and greets the crowd, letting us know in a booming voice that we are all "incredible" and "some of the best athletes in the world." I clap along with everyone else.

Mr. Mynt reminds us that this week isn't about pushing sales or posing for the cameras. "The real reason we're here is to give back. My team has lined up some truly incredible events for you to take part in. In about an hour, we have a VIP meet-and-greet scheduled with some of your biggest fans."

I shift in my seat, trying to hide my discomfort. I doubt I'm high up on the list of athletes that people are excited to see.

"And Christmas is right around the corner, so we also have a full offering of holiday-themed events, like breakfast with Santa, our polar plunge, our snowman- and cookie-decorating contests, and of course, *my* favorite event, the Merry Mynt Ball. This week is going to be packed full of fun, fun, fun!"

There's some more polite applause from the crowd. Those events don't sound too bad, except for the polar plunge. Jumping into a freezing-cold lake, pool, or wherever they hold the event is *not* my idea of fun. I shiver. Even though I'm an ice skater, I don't care for cold weather. Shocking, I know.

"But before all of that can happen, we need for all of you to get to know one another a little better. The Mynt Athletic Clothing family has grown since last year. For our festive ice breaker, we'll break out into small groups. You'll each say your name, your sport, a team if you have one, and answer a holiday question."

I sigh and try to keep from fidgeting. Hopefully I don't come off as too awkward. But I probably will. The only places I feel like myself are when I'm with friends, like Emma, or when I'm skating.

The second my blades hit the ice, the outside world blurs away. I don't think about who's watching or what they're expecting. It's just me and the music. But here? In this room full of accomplished athletes? I feel like I'm an imposter.

"And let's have you guys all get together," Mr. Mynt says cheerfully, waving toward my section of the room.

I plaster on a tight smile that hopefully reads as friendly and not mildly panicking and shuffle over to the group he's wrangled together. There are only four other people. I can do this.

The girl sitting to my left turns toward us with the kind of easy grin that reminds me of some of the sorority girls I used to see on campus at Fresno State. "Hi, I guess I'll go first. I'm Kelly and I'm a golfer." She looks over to the projector near the stage that has the list of questions. "If you were one of Santa's reindeer, which one would you be and why?"

It only takes her a second to answer. "Oh my goodness, that's easy. I would totally be Prancer because everyone loves watching me on the green and I always give a good show, bringing more viewers to the game of golf."

I nod politely, though my brain is scrambling to remember the other reindeer and a reason.

A snowboarder named Aspen Sterling goes next followed by another girl with a lot of energy. "Hi everyone, I'm Juliet Morgan, and I play soccer for the US women's team. And I guess if I had to pick a reindeer, I'd pick Rudolph, if that counts, because when I get cold, my nose turns bright-red."

Darn, why didn't I think of that? Rudloph would've been a great answer.

Then it's my turn. I clear my throat. "Um, hi." I hold up my hand in a half wave. "I'm Chloe Reynolds, and I'm a figure skater."

That part's easy. I glance at the screen again. The question is still glowing up there. What were the names of the reindeer again? And what did the others say? I rack my brain for an answer as I force a smile.

"And I guess . . . if I were one of Santa's reindeer, I'd be Blitzen." I pause, then rush to clarify. "Because like lightning, I tend to show up out of nowhere. Like at Nationals. I kind of won it by accident."

There's a beat of silence, then a few polite chuckles. I'm not sure if they think I'm joking. Either way, I'll take it.

The last person in our group is the guy who was sitting

near me. "I'm Holden Prescott. I play hockey, and I'm with the Minnesota Wolves."

Ha, I knew it. Hockey player. I can pick them out a mile away.

"If I had to be a reindeer . . . I'd be Comet because I'm fast on the ice."

Just as the words are out of his mouth, "Jingle Bells" bursts out of the speakers, cheerful and a little too loud, signaling that time's up.

Mr. Mynt pops back up onto the stage, grinning like he just handed out candy canes to a stadium full of kids. "All right, everyone, well done. Now we have just enough time for a group photo!"

There's a bit of shuffling as we're all herded forward toward the stage. Someone hands me a Santa hat that still has a tag attached, and I slip it on sideways. We squeeze in close, me between Holden and the girl who liked Prancer, and the photographer counts down. I smile.

"We got it." The photographer flashes a thumbs-up.

"Great," Mr. Mynt says. "Let's go spread some cheer. There's no pressure, just be as charming as a mug of peppermint cocoa."

A few minutes later, the doors open and the VIP ticket holders begin to fill the room. I take a deep breath and force a smile as the first few fans approach, but my mind drifts back to the hallway, to the puddle, to the look on Drew's face right before I ran.

"Oh my gosh, Chloe! I've been dying to meet you," a teenage girl says as she approaches me. "You're my favorite skater." Her dad hovers behind her, recording us with his phone.

I push my thoughts aside and turn my full focus to the girl in front of me. I'm reminded that I have work to do.

"Aww, thank you so much. You have no idea how much hearing you say that means to me. Are you an ice skater too?"

"Yeah. I just passed my junior moves test."

"Maybe I'll see you at Nationals this year." I wink and sign her badge.

She beams.

As she walks away, a younger girl approaches with her mom. I guess she's around eight or nine years old. Her hands tremble slightly as she cradles an ice skate to her chest.

I crouch a little to meet her at eye level. "Hi there, I'm Chloe. What's your name?"

"Brittany." She sheepishly hands the skate to me.

"And what's your favorite skating move?"

"Layback spins," she says, wide-eyed.

"You're brave. I always got scared looking up at the ceiling." We take a photo together, and I scribble my name on the skate, then hand it back to her. "It was nice meeting you."

"You too!"

She hugs me. As I watch her bounce away with a grin, my chest swells. Maybe I don't always feel like I belong in rooms like this, but to these girls, I do. I'm not just a skater. I'm someone worth looking up to. And for the first time all day, I start to believe it too.

When we're done, I slip away from the meet-and-greet crowd and head for the lobby, gripping a to-go cup. After crashing into Drew, this is the least I can do. I just hope he forgives me.

I retrace my steps from earlier. The mess has been cleaned from the floor, but Drew is still working on the fish tank. His sleeves are pushed up, and he's muttering something under his breath.

I hover for a second, unsure if now's a good time, or if I should run as fast as I can in the other direction. No. What am I thinking? Meeting Drew here earlier has to be a sign. I'm doing this. I clear my throat. "Hey."

He glances over his shoulder, brows raised. There's still a streak of green across his jaw that somehow makes him look even more infuriatingly attractive. "Hey, Chloe," he says. "You're back."

"I am."

He stands. "I didn't scare you away like the Grinch?"

"Not yet." I hold out the to-go cup. "I, um . . . brought you this. It's peppermint hot chocolate. Not quite an apology bouquet, but it's the thought that counts, right?"

Drew takes the cup and eyes it warily. "I hope you didn't put something like fish flakes in there instead of chocolate."

"I wouldn't do that," I say softly.

He chuckles. "I'm sorry, I couldn't resist. I know *you* wouldn't. But Emma might."

He chuckles and takes a sip. "Wow. This is really good."

I shrug. "I remembered you liked peppermint, and I figured . . . well, you looked like you could use a little pick-me-up."

"Seriously," he says, lowering the cup. "Thanks. You didn't have to do this."

"I wanted to," I say quickly. "Also, I may have felt bad about accidentally giving you a seaweed facial."

He grins. "To be fair, that was mostly on me."

I nod solemnly. We fall quiet for a second, and I

suddenly become very interested in the peppermint ribbon on a nearby garland.

"I should probably let you get back to the tank," I say, backing away slowly. "But . . . I'm glad you're not too mad."

He lifts the cup in a mock salute. "This helps."

"Phew." I give a dramatic exhale. "Guess I won't have to hide behind the gingerbread house for the rest of the week."

"Not unless you hit me with another bucket."

"Noted."

I turn, cheeks warm, and walk back toward the elevators with a little more spring in my step. Behind me, I hear him mutter, "Best apology I've ever tasted."

I grin all the way to my suite.

Chapter Six

DREW

When I arrive at the cafe, it's buzzing with people wearing lanyards. There must be a fitness convention taking place. Everyone here is in great shape, and their trays are full of healthy food that's high in protein. It makes me want to hit the gym—eventually. First, though, I'm not about to miss out on a free lunch.

I scan the room. Emma has grabbed a table near the back. She waves, and I start weaving my way through the crowd. But as I get closer, my steps falter. Chloe's with her. She looks up at the same time I do. Our eyes lock. Her expression flickers into a half smile. I feel that same off-balance tug I felt when she brought me that delicious peppermint hot chocolate.

Emma brightens when she spots me. "Drew! Good timing. Come sit."

I manage a nod, unable to speak.

"You remember Chloe, don't you?"

"I do. Thanks for the cocoa earlier," I say with a grin as I slide into the seat. "I think my blood sugar finally forgave you for the incident."

I didn't fully appreciate it when I first saw her, but Chloe is still gorgeous. Her hair's longer now. It falls just past her shoulders in soft, silky waves. A few golden highlights catch in the café's overhead lights. Have I ever seen her wear it down? In every memory I have of her, it's been twisted up into a bun or in a ponytail.

My brain jumps back in time three years to Emma's college graduation. I don't remember the ceremony too well, other than it felt like I was melting in the Fresno summer heat, but I remember the dinner.

We went to Emma's favorite place in Clovis—The Little Blue Caboose Bistro. Emma, Mom, and Dad were all buzzing with excitement. And then there was Chloe.

She was quiet the whole time and barely said more than five words to anyone. She smiled when it was expected and nodded during the conversations. But the rest of the time, she just picked at her food and looked sad.

Later, when we all drifted outside for group photos, I ended up next to her. At some point, she caught me staring.

"You can ask, you know," she said. "It won't bother me."

"Ask what?"

"Why my family isn't here."

I'd hesitated, unsure how to respond, but I didn't have to.

"They're in Monaco. Some fundraiser-slash-vacation thing. Graduation overlapped with their plans. They'd already booked their tickets and hotel and well . . . you know," she said softly.

I held back a wince. "They didn't even try to come?"

"They sent a very expensive flower arrangement and

some beautiful Cartier jewelry. Fresno State was never their plan for me. They had their hearts set on me attending an Ivy League school."

I couldn't stop myself from putting my foot in my mouth. "And you didn't because . . . ?"

"I wanted to take control of my life."

I remember just standing there, not knowing what to say to that. It was the kind of answer, however, that stayed with you long after the moment passed.

And it had. Even now, the memory still stirs anger inside of me. How could someone work that hard, graduate with honors, and still not be enough to make their parents show up? If I ever met her parents, they were going to get a piece of my mind. Even all these years later.

Back in the café, I focus on the ladies. Chloe's still seated across from Emma, sipping from her cup. Her eyes flicker toward me, then away again.

Most people would've walked away from the tank mess earlier without a second glance. But not Chloe. She came back to apologize because that's just the type of person she is. Kind and considerate.

I pull up a chair between the girls and nod toward the cookies they've been eating. There's a Christmas tree with little green sugar pearls, a snowman with a slightly crooked hat, and a snowflake. "Any of those got my name on it?"

"Nope. These are for us," Emma says, her hand hovering protectively over the plate.

I frown. "I thought you said you'd buy me lunch."

"I did, but I didn't buy these. Chloe did."

"Here," Chloe says, her voice quieter now. "Why don't you take the tree. It's mint chocolate chip. You're favorite."

A warmth creeps into my chest. She remembered my favorite drink earlier, and now she's remembered my favorite cookie. I feel embarrassed. I don't know what her favorite drink and cookie are. "Thanks," I tell her, softer than I mean to.

Chloe just shrugs, reaching for another cookie, and the moment passes. As I chew, I can't stop wondering what else she remembers or what else she notices. Which is ridiculous because the last thing I need right now is Emma's best friend lodged in my head.

Chapter Seven

CHLOE

As Drew reaches across the table, his fingers brush mine. The contact only lasts for a second, but it causes a hoard of sugarplum fairies to start fluttering inside my chest.

He's changed into some clean clothing. His sleeves are still rolled up to his forearms, revealing tan skin and strong wrists. His jaw is dusted with a day's worth of stubble, his lips full and a little chapped from the cold. For a moment, I wonder what it would be like to kiss them.

Then I remember where I am. Gah. Why am I even thinking about this right now? Something like that would *never* happen. To him, I'll always be Emma's mildly awkward and occasionally clumsy friend. I may be graceful on the ice, but off it, sometimes I have trouble walking in a straight line. And crashing into him today is further proof of that.

I take a long sip of my apple cider latte, trying not to let my mind wander too far, but with Drew sitting this close, I'm losing the battle.

"So what's your favorite cookie flavor?" he asks.

"The, um, same as yours. Mint chocolate chip." He presses his lips together thoughtfully.

"And your drink of choice?"

"A peppermint hot chocolate."

"Great minds think alike." He grins.

I nod.

Emma, who has been busy nibbling on a snowman cookie, raises an eyebrow. "Huh. Interesting. You two are twinning." She pauses thoughtfully. "You know, I always thought you would make a cute couple."

I choke slightly on my drink while Drew stiffens in surprise.

"What?" she says innocently. "I'm just saying. Stranger things have happened. It's the holidays." Emma's eyes ping-pong between us. "Anyway, fill me in. What happened earlier?"

"I was running late for today's athlete orientation and bumped into him. Literally. And I still feel awful about it."

"Uh-huh. So *that's* how the tank area became a swamp." Emma leans back in her chair, lips twitching with barely contained amusement. "At least this time it wasn't because you were clumsy."

I groan and bury my face in my hands. It's a running joke between us, how many times I've crashed, spilled, or tripped my way through life.

"Chloe? Clumsy?" Drew says with surprise. "Not possible. She's an ice skater."

"Oh, but I am," I say, laughing now. "I can land a triple on a blade thinner than a pencil, but if you put me in sneakers, I can't walk in a straight line. Ask Emma. She's got an entire highlight reel of me walking into doors, dropping dinner because I tripped over my own feet . . . the list goes on and on."

"She's not lying," Emma adds smugly. "You should've seen her trying to carry a tray of cocoa last Christmas. The tree never recovered."

I can feel the weight of Drew's gaze on me. I steal a glance at him from under my lashes. He's still smiling. The air between us shifts, as if there's electricity in it, like the kind you get ahead of an approaching storm.

I suddenly become very aware of how close he's sitting to me. The table isn't that wide. Our knees could probably touch if either of us moved just an inch.

"Good to know. Next time, I'll wear a helmet," he says, his voice low and teasing.

I smile, maybe a little too wide, and take another sip of my cider to hide it. "I should too. I'll add it to my packing list. Right after my skates and snacks."

"I'm glad you're still skating. You were always pretty good at it."

"Thanks," I say softly.

Emma snorts. "Chloe isn't just *good*. She's the national champion."

"You are?" Drew blinks a few times.

"Guilty as charged," I say.

He shoots me a surprised look. I try not to squirm. I'm used to people recognizing my name, not my face. Why does it matter so much to me what he thinks?

"Wow," he finally says. "That's seriously impressive."

"Thanks," I murmur even softer.

Emma checks her phone and stands abruptly. "Sorry, guys, but it looks like I've got to run back to the desk. I just got an SOS text from Neil. He's being swarmed."

"But Emma—" I start.

"I know, Chloe. I hate to run out on you guys, but I promise I'll make it up to you." She shrugs her blazer back on. "And don't worry, brother dearest, yes, I scored those Midnight Pepper tickets, *and* I'm still covering lunch. While you guys were talking, I made you a reservation over at the Mynt Society. It's the restaurant near the rink. Order what you want, and the guys can send me the bill. Just don't go *too* crazy." She stands and smirks at both of us. "And try not to make another pond."

She pops out the door, leaving me behind with Drew. Alone. "Well, I guess it's just us now," he says.

I reach for my latte again, even though it's nearly gone. My fingers wrap around the cup. Drew studies me. His expression is unreadable. "You'd think she would've come up with a better excuse than an SOS text," I tease, keeping the tone light.

"Agreed." He chuckles. "She's used that line on me before. But at least we're getting something out of it." He rubs his hands together. "The Mynt Society has the best steak in town. I'm so ordering the rib eye."

I let out another nervous laugh. We both stand. I shrug into my coat, my hands fumbling with the zipper. Drew opens the door, and we step outside together.

The snow has stopped falling. Our shoes crunch over the fresh powder as we head toward the path that winds around the rink and leads to the restaurant. The sun peeks out from behind the clouds.

"So," he says, shoving his hands into his coat pockets, "national champion, huh?"

I groan. "Are we really circling back to that?"

"Uh-huh. You're the best skater in America. That's kind of a big deal." He glances over at me with a smirk. "You always did skate circles around everyone else. Now I know why."

I nudge him lightly with my elbow. "I didn't know you paid that much attention," I say, trying to sound casual.

"I've always noticed you."

My pulse begins to race erratically. I open my mouth but can't form the right words. So instead I glance ahead to where the sign for The Mynt Society glows faintly.

"Wow," I say, clearing my throat. "Emma really doesn't mess around when it comes to lunch reservations."

The facade of the restaurant looks like a rustic lodge. Frosted windows glimmer with twinkling golden lights. A cluster of evergreen wreaths hangs over the double doors, trimmed with eucalyptus, myrtle, and sprigs of peppermint-printed ribbon.

Drew holds the door open for me. A blast of warm air hits my face as we enter. Inside, it takes a moment for my eyes to adjust, but I can just make out tables set with matte-gold flatware, and candles flickering in cut-glass holders. It's the kind of place that screams *expensive.*

He follows my gaze and grins. "You should see what she does when she's trying to impress someone."

I risk a sidelong look at him. "You think this was her way of impressing us with her mad skills as a concierge?"

"No," he says. "I think this was her way of trying to set us up."

I stiffen. "For what? A bank robbery?" I blurt out. What is going on in my brain right now? I can't stop putting my foot in my mouth. Of all the times for me to make a stupid remark.

He blinks, then smirks. "That's a new one." He cocks his head.

I groan and press a hand to my face. "That's not what I meant to say."

"Maybe not, but I like where your brain went." His

laugh is low and warm. "As you well know, my sister doesn't do subtle. She thinks I've been lonely and depressed since I was laid off from my job and moved home. Her solution is to help me find somebody to date."

I've never told Emma this, but I've had a crush on her brother since our sophomore year of college. I still remember when I realized how much I liked him. It started when Emma found me standing in the doorway of our dorm room right before winter break, clutching my phone tightly.

"Why do you look like somebody left a lump of coal in your stocking?" she'd asked me. "It's almost the end of the semester. That means five full weeks of free time!"

"I just found out the dorms are closed over the break."

"Okaaay. And that's a bad thing? It's not like anybody will be here."

"I was."

"You weren't gonna go home?"

I stared at the ground, not wanting to admit the truth. "No. My parents are doing a river cruise in Europe. I didn't want to be home alone."

"And they didn't invite you?"

"No, it's a twenty-one-and-over cruise."

Emma's jaw clenched at that.

Mom and Dad had offered to buy me a plane ticket to fly into Germany to spend Christmas Day with them when the boat docked in Cologne, but it felt like a waste. I wanted to spend a few weeks with them. Not a day.

If that was their offer, I'd rather be at home alone than in Europe. Don't get me wrong, I loved traveling as much as the next person, but not when it was ultra crowded. Or freezing cold.

"Oh well, I guess I'll just suck it up and go home to San Diego," I'd told Emma.

"You are not spending Christmas by yourself."

"It's fine. I'll pick up some treats at Trader Joe's and binge the Hallmark channel."

"There's another option," she said, eyes lighting up. "Come home with me."

"To Colorado?"

"Yes!" She nodded enthusiastically.

"I don't know. I wouldn't want to intrude."

"You wouldn't be. Mom and Dad would love to have you. It'll be just like it is here. We'll share my room, and I'll show you around Winterbrook. It'd be like I had a sister."

My had heart fluttered. Her words hit me like a snowball to the heart. That was one thing I'd always wanted. A sister.

Within minutes, she had her parents on speakerphone. And just like that, I was going to Colorado for Christmas. It was decided that Drew would drive us there. We could've flown, but the Sullivan siblings always preferred road trips.

Drew picked us up after our last final. His car smelled like pine and cinnamon, and there was a travel mug of hot chocolate already waiting in the cup holder for me.

"All right, ladies, ready to hit the road?" he asked.

"I call the back seat!" Emma yelled, tossing her bag in and flopping down.

Drew snorted. "Fine by me. I'd rather have Chloe as my co-pilot anyway."

Bubbles had fizzed inside my stomach as I slid into the front seat, trying not to overthink it. I thought Emma's brother was adorable when we met in Santa Monica. But seeing him again was proof positive he was a guy I'd totally try to score a date with if he weren't off-limits. Emma had never explicitly said anything, but it would be too awkward. He was a real adult, and I was just a college kid.

We drove for a few hours. Christmas lights blurred past in streaks of color. At some point, Emma passed out in the back, curled up, and started snoring as loud as a hibernating bear. It was just me and Drew and the long, dark road.

I'd been nervously fiddling with my hoodie strings for twenty minutes, trying to think of something smart to say, when he broke the silence.

"Are you always this quiet when it's late?" he asked, his voice low.

"Only when I don't know what to say," I admitted, not sure why I was sharing this with him.

He glanced at me and smiled. "You don't need to say anything." A few minutes passed. Then he said, "You're different than I expected."

I tilted my head. "Different how?"

He kept his eyes on the road, but there was a small, thoughtful pause before he answered. "I don't know yet. We didn't spend a lot of time together in LA, but hmm . . ."

"I'm just Emma's friend. And a figure skater." I stared out the window into the darkened sky.

"No, Chloe, you're much more than that. According to my sources, you're also a math whiz."

I pressed my hand to my mouth. He chanced another glance at me, and the little twitch at the corner of his lips told me he was proud of himself for making me smile.

"You know . . ." he said, drumming his fingers lightly on the steering wheel, "we've still got a couple hours to go. It might be just enough time for me to unlock all your deepest, darkest secrets. Want to play twenty questions?"

"Only if I get to ask first."

He grinned. "Deal. Hit me."

I tapped my finger against my knee like I was seriously pondering the world's most important mystery. "Okay. What's your favorite Christmas movie?"

He groaned. "You're not easing into this at all, are you?"

"Come on. Everybody has a favorite movie," I teased. "Just don't say it's *Die Hard*."

He gave me a mock offended look. "*Die Hard* is a cult classic."

"But is it romantic?"

"You like those cheesy, romantic Christmas movies like Emma, don't you?" he guessed.

"I like when people find each other," I said softly, turning to look out the window. "Especially during the holidays. Something about this time of year makes me believe it's still possible."

He didn't answer right away. Just shifted his hand on the steering wheel and looked over at me again. "Me too," he finally said. "This is classified information, but my favorite is the claymation *Rudolph the Red-Nosed Reindeer*. The one with Burl Ives."

"Really?"

He nodded solemnly. "There's something about a scrappy little reindeer with a shiny nose that just gets me every time."

"Well, your secret is safe with me, Comet."

"Of all Santa's reindeers, why am I Comet?"

"Because," I said, pretending to think very seriously, "Comet always flies a little ahead of the others. He's very underrated."

He raised an eyebrow, clearly amused. "Do you think I'm underrated?"

I shrugged, biting back a smile. "You're a classic."

"I'll take that."

We kept playing. We asked one another favorites, would-you-rathers, and a few "What's the most embarrassing thing you've ever done" questions, which I regretted immediately. But I didn't stop.

Outside the window, the snow started falling heavier, slow and steady in the glow of the headlights. But I barely noticed. Because there in the car, with Drew's voice low and his smile turning soft at the edges, it felt like something was shifting. The air between us wasn't just friendly anymore. Drew made me feel seen. And for the first time in a long time, I was happy.

And now, here I am. Alone again with Drew. Emma's teased me about setting us up in the past, but I never actually thought she'd follow through with it. I don't know whether I should kill her or thank her.

<h1 style="text-align:center">Chapter Eight</h1>

DREW

The hostess leads us to a cozy table near the bar. I pull out Chloe's chair, then take a seat opposite her. The table's already set, with menus tucked neatly into crisp linen napkins and water glasses settled onto gold-rimmed coasters.

I glance across at Chloe. She's fiddling with her silverware, lining up the fork and knife. Her cheeks are a little flushed, probably from the cold. Or from the whole "setup" thing I just dropped.

I know I shouldn't have said that. But it's the truth. Emma doesn't do subtle. The thing is, my sister's not wrong about me. At times lately, I *have* been a little depressed. The life I was building outside of Winterbrook went up in flames. Coming back here felt like a neon sign flashing "failure."

The server drops off a basket of rosemary rolls, and a pair of tiny bowls filled with whipped butter. I grab a roll and tear it open, letting the steam warm my hands. My gaze shifts back to Chloe.

She really is beautiful, and shines from the inside out.

I'm sure she could grace the cover of any magazine she wanted. But what I love about her is that she's not trying to impress anyone. She's just . . . well, herself. Today, she's wearing minimal makeup. Her hair is in a ponytail, and she's bundled in a black puffer vest over a white long-sleeve shirt.

But that's not what keeps pulling my focus. It's her. The way she lights up when she talks, especially about the skating lesson she gave earlier. She might be shy, but there's this quiet fire in her when she speaks. Her eyes are glowing. Not with pride in herself, but in the students. She really cares about everyone around her.

She's humble too. Chloe doesn't throw around the fact that she's a national champion. If anything, she tends to shy away from the spotlight. Winning hasn't changed her. She's still the same down-to-earth person I met at the Santa Monica Pier. I'd love to be someone she could lean on. But deep down, I'm not sure I'm good enough for her.

"So, um . . . *are* you lonely?" Chloe asks, placing her napkin on her lap.

I glance up from the roll in my hands, caught off guard. She's not fishing or making conversation just for the heck of it. She's asking because she wants to know.

I lean back slightly in my chair and give a half shrug. "Yeah. Sometimes," I admit. "Especially this time of year. The holidays are all about family and spending time with the people you love. Which I do, more than I'd like. I mean, I live with my parents and my sister. And I work for them. But I'd like to have some space and someone I can spend time with outside the family bubble."

She nods. "I get that. It's the same for me. I have my skating family back in Sequoia Valley, but sometimes I wish there was someone else in the picture. I don't want my entire life to revolve around skating. It'd be nice to have a break from it every now and then."

I glance at her, struck by how honest that is. Considering her parents once skipped her graduation to go jet setting, I wouldn't be surprised if she spent most of her childhood with nannies and rotating babysitters.

Even now, the way she says "skating family" makes me think that deep down, she's still on her own. And yet, I bet she never complains. In all the time I've known her, she's always carried herself with this quiet inner strength. I wish I were as strong as she is.

I tear off a piece of rosemary roll and dip it into the butter, glancing over just as Chloe does the same. Her cheeks are a soft, wintery pink—the exact shade you'd paint on a Nutcracker doll. I wish I could help her and make her feel a little less lonely.

"If you ever need a break from the skating world, someone who doesn't ask about triple Axels or talk about winning the Olympics, I volunteer as tribute," I say.

She glances up. Her eyelids flutter. "Thanks," she says quietly. Then, almost as if she needs something to focus on, she cracks open her menu. "You know, the offer works both ways. I'm around if you ever need a friend too."

My stomach twists in knots at hearing her words. Chloe isn't just being polite. She means it.

A sudden realization hits me—maybe the reason no one else measures up is because I've been comparing them to her all along. All the women I've dated, like the one lecturing me about carbon footprints, and the influencer who was glued to her phone chasing the perfect reel, always left me wishing they were more like Chloe. She's easygoing, genuine, and the kind of person who, like me, would pick a burger-and-milkshake joint over a stuffy rooftop wine bar for dinner.

I take a deep breath, pretending to study the menu since I already know I'm going to order the rib-eye steak. Across the table, Chloe is flipping through hers, her brows scrunched in concentration.

I'm not really looking for a girlfriend right now. As it is, my life is a half-unpacked suitcase that's still stuck in the hallway. I don't know what I'm doing next or where I'll land, or if I'll land at all.

But compared to the women I've dated lately, Chloe's in a different league. She's funny, kind, and genuine. When I *am* ready to date, I want somebody exactly like her.

I steal another glance at her. She's tucked a strand of hair behind her ear. Her eyes are flicking over the menu. There's a small crease between her brows like she's working something out in her head. I get the sense she's not just thinking about lunch.

She sets her menu down and looks at me, a little hesitant. "I've been thinking . . . would you be willing to hang out with me at a few of the events this week? Nothing major. I just figured since Emma's going to be working most of the time, and I know you get off earlier from work than she does, that it might be nice to have someone I know around. A friend."

My pulse increases. Has she been reading my mind? I raise an eyebrow, trying to play it cool. "A friend, huh? Is this a strategic snack-sharing alliance, or are you just after my sparkling conversation?"

"Nothing like that." She draws a few circles on the tablecloth with her fingers. "I . . . I don't feel like I belong here."

"Don't belong?"

She tilts her head toward the bar. "There are so many famous athletes here. I'm not exactly on their level."

"Chloe, I thought everyone with lanyards was just really into CrossFit until just now. I'm the worst person to ask about celebrities. But I'll tell you this—You *do* belong here. Don't sell yourself short." I shake my head. "If I tag along with you, do I get a name tag or a commemorative tote bag?"

She glances down like she's not sure whether to believe me, and something about that look hits me harder than I expect. She really doesn't see what the rest of us do—how insanely talented and driven she is. I want to say more, to tell her she's impressive and a role model, but the words stick in my throat.

Her body relaxes. "I can't make any promises on a tote bag, but I can probably get you some free snacks."

I pump my fist. "I'll take it."

<h1 style="text-align:center">Chapter Nine</h1>

CHLOE

The next morning, I start my day by skating on what's hands down one of the most picturesque rinks I've ever been to. There's a stunning backdrop of snow-dusted mountains and the faint smell of cinnamon and pine drifting from the nearby cocoa stand. It's all so magical! For the first time since I've arrived at the Mynt Peak Resort, I feel relaxed.

The rink has always been the place I go to clear my head. It's a space where everything slows down, and my body knows what to do even when my brain doesn't. Which is ironic, considering how cluttered my thoughts are right now.

Instead of focusing on the lesson I'll be giving to some of the resort's guests a little later today, I stroke around the rink's perimeter, mentally replaying every word from yesterday's lunch with Drew. He agreed to spend the week with me. Just as friends. No big deal.

Except it kind of *is* a big deal. Because I've had a crush on him since forever, and now he's going to be spending time with me. On purpose. I half expected him to laugh at me. I didn't even plan to ask. The words just slipped out. But if I'm being completely honest, I'm glad they did.

Because this? It feels a little bit like the beginning of a fairy tale. I know I shouldn't get carried away. But deep down, there's a tiny flickering hope that maybe, just maybe, by the end of the week, he'll see me the same way I've always seen him.

My mind jumps back to the night we met. Emma and I were in LA, spending the week playing tourists during spring break at the end of our freshman year.

We were trying to take a selfie at the Santa Monica Pier when a voice said from behind us, "You guys need a person with longer arms to take that for you if you wanna fit the whole boardwalk in."

I lowered my phone and turned, already mentally prepared to give the guy a "No thanks" and tell him that was one of the lamest pickup lines I'd ever heard. The guy was wearing a Pacific Skyways hoodie, athletic shorts, and aviator sunglasses. I had to admit, he was attractive. But that was beside the point.

My hands went to my hips. "Uh, thanks for the offer, but we don't need your—"

"Drew!" Emma squealed, launching herself at him. She jumped up, wrapping her arms and legs around his body. He caught her and spun her around like they did this all the time.

I frowned. This was supposed to be a girls' trip, not a couple's trip. I didn't even know Emma had a boyfriend. I thought she was single, like me. How long had she been keeping him a secret?

Once Emma's feet were back on the ground, she grinned and gestured toward me. "Chloe, come meet Drew, my brother."

I relaxed. This was Drew? Huh. She made it seem like he was a skinny, string-bean guy with pale skin from spending all his time indoors playing video games. But he wasn't. He reminded me of one of those stereotypical California surfers.

Drew was about a foot taller than Emma. About five foot ten. He had golden sun-kissed skin and nutmeg-colored hair with a few blond highlights. He wasn't super muscular-looking, like the guys we saw on Venice Beach, but he wasn't a stranger to working out either. His legs had some definition to them.

Drew pulled down his sunglasses just enough to give me a look over the top of them. They were a warm honey color. His smile was teasing. As I looked closer, the family resemblance was obvious. He and Emma might have different-colored eyes and hair, but they had the same playful energy. "So, you're *the* Chloe. Emma talks about you all the time."

"Oh. Uh. Cool," I mumbled, completely losing track of what I was supposed to say. For all my friend had talked about her brother, she hadn't actually given me too many details on him.

Emma punched his arm lightly. "You said you were too busy and too important to hang out with us!"

"I decided to make an exception," he said with a shrug.

She narrowed her eyes. "How did you even know where we were?"

"Location sharing on your phone. You didn't disable it. Rookie move." He flashed a grin like he'd just outwitted a spy network.

Emma groaned. "Creep."

"You mean genius," he corrected smoothly, sliding his sunglasses back on. "And besides, I figured I'd be the best possible tour guide. LA is my hometown." I tried not to stare at his arms as he gestured dramatically to the pier.

"At least someone will appreciate my efforts," he added with a wink in my direction.

My cheeks flushed. I was sure they were lobster-red. "I'm just here for the churros," I muttered, quickly looking away.

"Spoken like a girl after my own heart," Drew said in a way that made my stomach flip. "Don't worry, I'll make sure you get the best ones. Not the expensive tourist-trap ones that taste like freezer burn and cardboard."

Emma looped an arm around my shoulder. "Chloe's from San Diego, which is like three hours from here. I'm sure they have better churros down there. But if you want to show us where to grab dinner on our broke-college-girl budget, we won't say no."

"I'll do you one better," Drew said, slinging an arm around his sister and steering us toward the street. "Dinner is on me."

Emma threw her hands in the air. "Yes! That means I can splurge and get a double chocolate-chip frappuccino with extra whip from Norma's Cafe for breakfast tomorrow!"

Drew chuckled. "Wait until you two graduate and get real jobs as concierges at high-end hotels, then you can drink overpriced foam every day."

"Drew," she groaned. "Get your facts right. I've told you before, Chloe isn't studying hospitality management like me. She's smart. She's a math major. And she won't need a real job. She's a figure skater who's gonna go pro when we graduate."

"Figure skater, huh?" Drew turned to me, cocking a brow. "So you do spinny things on ice?"

I rubbed the back of my neck. "That's one way to put it."

Emma gave him a look like, "I can't believe you said something that stupid." She sighed dramatically. "Ignore him. I got all the brain cells in the family."

Drew groaned. "You're lucky Chloe is here, otherwise your dinner would be gas-station hot dogs and a bag of chips."

"Yuck." Emma scrunched her face. "Everybody knows that's one food you should avoid."

"What's wrong with gas-station hot dogs?"

"Don't get me started," she muttered.

"I'm genuinely curious, sister dearest. Now tell me . . . what's wrong with them?"

I laughed, finally relaxing.

Somehow, in the span of fifteen minutes, Drew had gone from the random guy in aviators to someone who made me feel like I belonged. Like I wasn't just Emma's quiet roommate tagging along on a trip.

I remember thinking that for the first time in my life, I felt like I wasn't the awkward third wheel. Don't get me wrong, I love my parents, and I know they've always wanted what was best for me, but for so much of my life, they were too busy for me. Emma and Drew, on the other hand, treated me like one of their siblings. I felt like I belonged.

And speaking of Drew . . . just as I skate over to the boards to grab my water bottle, I spy him leaning casually against the rink rail with a coffee in hand, his gaze fixed firmly on me.

"Hey," he says, lifting the cup slightly in greeting.

I nod to him, take a drink from my bottle, then skate over. "Hi. You're here early. I didn't think I'd see you until later."

"I had a delivery to drop off. And I also wanted to check on the fish tank."

"And how's it doing since yesterday's deep cleaning?"

"Better," he says, rubbing the back of his neck. "But I still need to replace part of the filtration system and the, uh . . . never mind. It's aquarist stuff. I don't want to bore you."

I tilt my head. "If I wasn't interested, I wouldn't have asked."

He blinks, then a slow smile creeps across his face. It's a look that sends a shiver of delight up my spine.

I take another sip of water. "How much time do you have on your hands?"

He glances at his watch. "I can spare a half hour."

The wheels in my head start to spin. Here's my chance to spend some time with Drew! And introduce him to my world. "Perfect. That's just enough time to squeeze in a skating lesson."

He inhales sharply. "I run, I ski, and I snowboard. But I'm not coordinated enough for ice skating."

I cross my arms and raise an eyebrow. "When was the last time you tried?"

"Uh . . . I don't know."

"If you don't remember, then it's time to try again." I gesture toward the empty rink. "Who knows when we'll have private ice again?"

His gaze shifts to the rink, then back to me. There's a split second where I think he might back out, but then he sighs. "I wear size nine in skates."

Internally, I'm doing my happy dance. "I'll see what I can find."

Chapter Ten

DREW

I knew it was a long shot, taking the scenic route from the convention center back to the delivery van just for a chance to catch a glimpse of Chloe. But today, luck was on my side. She was out on the rink skating alone. And man, is she like a swan out there. Even though she was just skating in slow circles, I couldn't take my eyes off her.

I probably looked like a total creeper lingering near the rail, inching closer for a better view. But I didn't care. After spending the morning running around like a headless reindeer delivering trees and arrangements, I figured I'd earned a few minutes for myself.

I glance down at the skates in my hands and exhale. The deliveries are going to be behind schedule after this, and I really hope my parents don't notice. Technically, I shouldn't have agreed to this skating lesson. But the second Chloe asked, I wanted to say yes. I want to be near her.

Last night, I went down a Chloe rabbit hole watching competition videos and old interviews. I didn't mean to stalk her, exactly. I just couldn't stop watching. And sometime between one and two in the morning, when she was talking to an interviewer about why she wears mismatched socks before a competition—for superstition reasons—I realized that my feelings for Chloe run way deeper than I thought.

As I finish tying the laces of the rental skates together, I glance up and find her biting back a giggle. "What?"

"You, um, aren't supposed to wrap the laces around the boot if they're too long," she says, failing to contain the laughter any longer.

I blow out air. This is exactly why I didn't want to skate in the first place. I'm already making a fool of myself. "What *are* you supposed to do?"

"You tie them normally. They should be tight, but comfortable. Then you tuck the ends into the skate."

I glance skyward. "Somebody needs to invent skates with Velcro."

"They exist."

"Then why don't I get to use a pair?"

"Because they're usually for kids. They're not sturdy enough for adults." She steps off the ice and toward the bench where I'm sitting. "Do you mind if I help?"

I shrug, trying not to look too grateful. "Knock yourself out."

She kneels in front of me, and her hands move fast and confidently. "How many thousands of times have you done this?" I ask.

"Hmm . . ." She glances up at me. "Well, I started skating when I was five. So if we multiply that by three times a week until I was ten, then bump that up to four practices a week, plus lessons twice a day . . ."

I groan. "Right. I forgot you were a math major."

She grins as she goes back to tightening the skates.

"Let's round up and just say the number's somewhere close to ten thousand times."

"I've always wondered, why *did* you pick math?"

"I thought I'd become a high school math teacher when I was done with skating. It's my favorite subject and I love being around kids." In less than a minute, she's done. She gives the laces one final tug and leans back, looking satisfied. "Alrighty. Looks like you're all set."

I watch her for a beat longer than I probably should. Of course she'd want to become a teacher. It's so Chloe. She's always thinking about how she can give back. She doesn't just skate circles around people. She outshines them. It makes me fall for her even more.

I stand. My legs wobble like spaghetti noodles, but somehow, I manage to follow Chloe onto the ice without face-planting. It's a small victory, but I'll take it.

She skates backward in front of me. "Not bad. But you need to loosen up. A band of ninjas isn't going to pop out and attack you. Bend your knees. Relax your shoulders."

"It won't be ninjas taking me out today. It'll be gravity." As if on cue, my skate catches on a rough patch and I stumble, arms flailing.

Before I hit the ice, Chloe loops her arm through mine and steadies me. Her fingers wrap around my sleeve, and I swear I feel a spark of electricity shooting straight through me. My breath catches.

"Good thing you're not wearing figure skates," she says lightly. "Otherwise, the toe picks would've sent you flying."

I glance down with a frown. "Toe picks? That doesn't sound hygienic."

She snorts. "Not a literal thing to pick dirt out of your toes. I'm talking about this thing." She points to the sharp, jagged metal at the front of her skate blade. "We use them for jumps and spins."

My eyes travel to my skates. They don't look like any skates I remember using. "Mine don't look like yours. Or have that thing."

"That's because they're hockey skates. I thought they'd be easier for you to start with. The boot isn't as stiff, and the blade is rounded."

"Oh, gotcha." That's another dumb thing I've said. It should've been obvious they're a different kind of skate than hers.

"Drew, don't be embarrassed. It's totally normal to not know the difference." She giggles.

I shift my weight, trying to find the right balance. "Okay, I think I've got it this time," I say, focusing hard as I even out over the blades. Chloe lets go of my arm, and although I'm glad I'm balancing on my own, I miss the warmth of her hand in mine. I push forward a few strokes. I'm wobbly but still upright. I glance at her for approval. "How am I doing, Coach?"

"You're skating like a champ."

I pump my fist in mock victory. "Does that mean I'm ready for a . . ." I rack my brain, trying to remember what the commentators called some of Chloe's jumps last night. "Quadruple Lutz?"

"Not yet, but maybe after a few more lessons, we can try a bunny hop." She laughs. "For now, we'll stick to gliding forward."

Oof. There goes my ego. "Brutal."

We fall into an easy rhythm, slowly circling the rink. My movements are still stiff, but each lap feels a little less like a disaster waiting to happen.

Chloe looks at me. "I've been meaning to ask . . . Why

were you working on the aquarium yesterday?"

"Oh, Emma asked me to. She knows I won't turn down a fish in need. I've been into aquascaping since I was a kid."

Chloe tilts her head. "Aqua-what?"

"You know . . ." I gesture vaguely in front of me. "Designing fish tanks to look like little underwater worlds. Coral, plants, driftwood, rocks. Think interior design, but for fish."

"That sounds awesome."

"It is." I grin. "Growing up, there was this little aquarium shop in downtown Winterbrook run by a guy named Mr. Ray," I say as we continue skating side-by-side. "I was obsessed with the place. Every time we were anywhere near downtown, I'd beg my mom to let me stop by. I couldn't get enough of the tanks and all the colorful fish. It felt like stepping into a different world."

She glances at me, intrigued.

"We went so often that Mr. Ray adopted me as his honorary grandson. On weekends, Mom would drop me off and I'd spend the day with him. He'd explain things to me like how the tanks worked, how to keep the pH of the water balanced, and which fish got along as community fish. Keeping aquariums became my hobby. And when I was old enough, he gave me my first real job."

"You were getting private lessons in fishkeeping as a kid," she teases. "That's kind of adorable."

"Mr. Ray was an amazing man. I was sad when he retired and moved to Denver. None of his kids wanted to take it over, so unfortunately, it went out of business." I sigh. "The only way to get fish nowadays is to order online or drive out to Vail or Denver."

There's a beat of silence between us, filled only by the sound of our skates cutting softly across the ice. "It's too bad somebody else hasn't opened a new shop," Chloe says.

"Yeah." My chest tightens a little. "If someone ever opened a new place, I wouldn't mind working there. It'd beat my parents' shop. I mean, it's not the worst, but I'm allergic to half the inventory."

"That sucks." Chloe wrinkles her nose. "Emma mentioned what happened with Pacific Skyways. I'm so sorry. Do you miss it?"

"Yes and no. I miss living in LA. The weather, the food, the beach, and the aquarium stores were all great." I force a smile. "But the job? Not so much. It paid well, but it was mind-numbingly boring. Half my department barely did anything. I could take a four-hour lunch break, and no one would notice."

Chloe's expression softens, and I suddenly feel exposed. I glance away, pretending to focus on my feet. "Getting laid off was a blow, but now that I've had more time to think about it, it was also a huge relief. It gave me the perfect excuse to walk away."

"Have you thought about what you want to do next?"

"A little. I know I don't want another corporate job. I want to do something with my creative side. But other than that, no. I've spent a little time looking through some job sites, but for the most part, I've been hoping something would just fall into my lap. But so far, it hasn't. It's up to me to take the bull by the horns and get going. After New Year's, I'll start searching more seriously for something." I sigh. "Sorry for turning this into a therapy session. This is not what you signed up for. Feel free to charge me by the hour."

She smiles softly. "You're not the only one whose plans got flipped upside down, you know. I haven't told this to anyone, but I was actually planning to retire from competitive skating after Nationals and join the touring company Dreams on Ice."

That throws me. "Retire? But you're only twenty-three."

"I am," she says slowly. "But figure skaters don't have long careers. We peak early, kind of like gymnasts. Before this year, the best finish I'd ever had at Nationals was fifth place. With all the up-and-coming juniors, I figured by next season, I'd be lucky to crack the top ten."

"So you wanted to go out on a high note?" I guess.

She nods. "Uh-huh."

I pause. "But then you won."

"Exactly." Her face falls. "And now everything's about training for the Olympics, fulfilling obligations for my sponsors, and putting in media appearances. I should be thrilled, right? But sometimes it still feels like this is somebody else's path. Like any second, someone's going to come over, tap me on the shoulder, and say, 'Oops. Sorry. We picked the wrong girl.'"

I shake my head. "Chloe, no. You earned that win. It wasn't luck. You've worked your butt off to get where you are."

"You sound like Emma," she says with a knowing smile.

"We *are* related."

She laughs softly. "Fair." Then her expression shifts. "Anyway, what I was trying to say is sometimes the paths we end up on aren't always the ones we imagine." Her gaze meets mine. "As cliché as this sounds, you'll know what's right for you when it's time. I don't think you should be in a rush. Figure out what you truly want to do."

"Thanks," I murmur. "That means more than you know."

She gives a tiny nod, then clears her throat and nudges my elbow lightly. "Okay, sentimental break's over," she jokes, though there's still softness in her tone. "Let's get back to your lesson. Relax more. You're still skating like a two-by-four."

I let out a short laugh. "Yes, Coach Chloe."

She holds out her hand, and I take it without hesitation. We skate the next lap together, and she talks me through how to do a forward crossover. Her voice is warm and patient. I can't help but feel like something has shifted between us. And I wonder if maybe I should push everything aside and ask her out on a date. Would she even say yes?

Chapter Eleven

CHLOE

"Thank you so much, Chloe!" says Nicole, a little girl in a red puffer coat and matching beanie, as I finish signing her skate.

"You're so welcome." I smile and stand, capping my Sharpie as she beams up at me.

"Are you giving lessons again tomorrow?" her mom asks as she helps Nicole unlace her skates.

"I am."

"Yesss!" Nicole squeals.

Her mom laughs. "We'll register for another session with the front desk. Hopefully there's still space available."

"If they say it's full, let them know I said it was okay to add you guys. They can call me if there's a problem."

"Thank you so much. We really appreciate it. Nicole has been talking about skating with you since we found out we'd be coming here."

My heart warms. "I'll see you then."

All of the kids I worked with today were part of a special group—families who won an all-expenses-paid trip to the resort through the Mynt to Make a Difference charity by having the children write essays about what the holidays mean to them.

These kids have been the highlight of my trip. They're eager, bright, and so excited about life. I make a mental note to ask the event coordinator if I can read some of the winning entries later. I want to know their stories. They deserve to be heard.

As I leave the rink and enter the lobby, I catch a whiff of the resort's signature mulled-wine scent. I drift past the garland-wrapped banisters and crackling fireplace, pausing when I see that the armchairs nestled between the grand tree and fireplace are empty. The quiet hum of distant holiday music filters through the lobby.

My legs ache and my back is sore, but it's the good kind of tired. This spot feels like the perfect place to sit and relax. I don't feel like being alone in my room right now. I sink into the nearest chair and let out a deep, contented sigh. The cushions are so soft. I close my eyes, soaking in the sound of the crackling fire.

My thoughts drift to Drew. Teaching him to skate this morning was surprisingly fun. He wasn't a natural, and I genuinely thought he might face-plant at least three different times, but he kept trying, kept laughing, and let me see a side of himself I've never seen before.

I open my eyes and take out my phone. Surprisingly, there's a text from my mom.

Mom: Just saw a tagged photo of you
on the resort's social feed. Hope
whatever event you're doing is going
well. I put some money in your account.
Buy yourself something fun for
Christmas. Let's talk sometime this
week. Just be warned Dad and I may
have spotty cell service. X

I reread Mom's message until the screen dims. I try not to think too much about Christmas. I'll be spending it alone this year. Again. Mom and Dad didn't even ask me if I wanted to join them on their Caribbean cruise.

They just assumed I would be too busy training for Nationals in January like I usually am. But if they'd asked, I would've made an exception this year. It'd be nice to spend some time with them. We haven't spent more than a few days together in years.

Growing up, I wondered at times if they even wanted me. We were never a traditional family. I spent more time with my nanny than I did with them. She's the one who attended my school recitals and skating competitions, and remembered my birthday.

Even when I won Nationals, Mom and Dad only sent flowers. When I graduated college, they sent jewelry. But they've never sent themselves.

It shouldn't still hurt. But it does. Even now, I find myself wanting to be chosen. Not out of obligation, but because someone *wants* to show up for me.

The sad thing is, it also happened with my first serious boyfriend, a swimmer named Nick, when he was supposed to be at Nationals in San Jose five years ago. He was the first guy I ever really let in. He said I'd always be a priority, and I foolishly believed him. I'd trained extra hard that year, and I couldn't wait to show him what I could do. Practices went well that week. I was nailing every jump, and skating better than I ever had.

Then the night of the short program arrived, and when I looked up in the stands, there was only Emma.

As much as I told myself I wouldn't let his absence get to me, it did. I fell on both my double Axel and triple flip and essentially took myself out of the competition. It was my worst finish at Nationals. Ever.

When I texted Nick later that night, he was still back in Fresno. He told me he had forgotten "my thing" and gone out for a buddy's birthday.

Nick chose his friends over me. His own *girlfriend*. I didn't matter. After that, I stopped expecting people to show up. And stopped wanting to date. It hurt less. I'm the only person I can count on. And maybe Emma and her family. They've always been so kind to me and made me feel like one of their own.

I pick up my phone, fingers hovering. I don't have the energy to text Mom. Instead, I text Drew.

> Chloe: Do you feel like joining me for the Cocoa and Christmas Tales event tonight?

> Drew: That depends.

> Chloe: On?

> Drew: What the story is.

I swipe out of our text chain and pull up the schedule of activities.

Chloe: It doesn't say, but it's probably
something like "The Night Before
Christmas" and "The Polar Express."

Drew: Will there be snacks?

I shake my head. He's all about the food.

Chloe: Yes, but it's dessert.

Drew: That's good enough for me.

Chloe: *Thumbs-up emoji.* It starts at
seven.

Drew: I'll see you then.

I tuck my phone away, heart a little lighter at the thought of spending more time alone with him, and wondering if I'll have the excuse to use him as a human armrest. Will his touch ignite another spark inside me? I guess there's only one way to find out.

At quarter to seven, Drew sends me a text.

Drew: I'm here and dressed to impress.

I raise an eyebrow. What exactly does he mean by that? I glance down at my green sweater dress and ankle boots. It's cute, but casual. A wave of doubt creeps in. Have I missed the mark again?

Chloe: Great. I'm in the lobby, outside
the fireside lounge.

Drew: On my way.

I barely have time to second-guess myself again before he appears. And he is *definitely* dressed to impress. Just not in the way I'd imagined.

He's wearing a red-and-white sweater that features a dachshund in a Santa hat building a snowman. Around his neck, there's a flashing LED necklace with red, green, blue, and yellow Christmas bulbs. Completing the ensemble is a pair of glowing reindeer antlers.

I press a hand to my mouth, torn between laughter and awe. "Wow. That's a . . . very festive look."

He groans and pinches the bridge of his nose. "You can thank Emma. She stole all my clothes while I was in the shower and left this masterpiece hanging on the doorknob."

I try to hold back a grin. "Wait. *All* your clothes?"

He nods solemnly. "She even emptied my closet and all my dresser drawers. It was either this or show up shirtless."

Bummer. I wouldn't have minded that look at all. But it *is* snowing outside, and I wouldn't want him to freeze. I bite the inside of my cheek and manage to ask, "And she did this because . . .?"

"I made the mistake of telling her I was meeting up with you tonight." He gives me a flat look. "I assume she wanted to be sure I left a lasting impression."

I laugh, the last of my outfit worries evaporating. "I'd say it's mission accomplished."

He bows slightly, the antlers wobbling. "Glad I could deliver." Then he straightens up and pulls out a small green gift bag from behind his back. It contains bright-red tissue and a candy cane sticking out of the side. "Here. This is for you."

"Oh, Drew . . ." I start, heart fluttering a little. "You really didn't have to—"

"I didn't," he cuts in sheepishly. "It's from Emma."

I blink. "Of course it is." I reach into the bag, the tissue paper crackling as I pull out a pair of blinking LED reindeer antlers and a matching bulb necklace for me. I can't help but laugh. "Oh, Emma," I say, shaking my head. "I'm glad we're going for subtle."

Drew smirks. "You say that like you're not impressed by how committed I am to the bit."

Oh, I'm impressed. Not just because he's here, rocking blinking antlers and a dachshund sweater, but because he's here for me. He could've canceled on me after Emma's little prank, but he didn't.

I put on the antlers and drape the necklace over my head. "There. Now we're officially matching. How do I look?"

He tilts his head, examining me with mock seriousness. "Great, except they're a little crooked. May I?"

"Sure."

He steps closer. My breath catches. His fingers brush lightly against my hair as he adjusts the antlers, and it's like flipping a switch. Every nerve ending sparks to life. I go completely still. My heart thuds loudly.

"You wore your hair down," he murmurs, fingers lingering a half-second too long. "It's a good look for you."

I swallow hard. "Thanks."

The air between us shifts. He's still so close, I can feel the faint brush of his breath. His hand hovers near my cheek now, suspended in midair. His gaze drops to my lips, and my pulse spikes.

A flurry is taking place inside my body like a snow globe shaken too hard. I've spent years convincing myself Drew Sullivan would never look at me like this. But tonight, it feels like I've made a flying leap forward. I *want* him to lean in and meet me halfway.

But the moment falls away as his hand drops. He takes a quick step back. "Come on," he says softly, clearing his throat. "They're probably waiting for us inside."

"You're right."

Drew pulls the door open and places a hand at the small of my back as we head toward the lounge. It's warm and cozy inside. The air smells like cinnamon, toasted marshmallows, and the faintest hint of peppermint.

Twinkling lights hang from the ceiling beams like starlight. Oversized pillows and fleece blankets are scattered around the fireplace, where a man in a red flannel shirt and jeans flips through a storybook, prepping for the event.

We make a beeline for the refreshment table. Drew grabs two ceramic mugs off a warming tray. There are at least six oversized dispensers labeled in loopy silver handwriting: *Hot Chocolate*, *White Chocolate*, *Peppermint Hot Chocolate*, *Mr. Mynt's Signature Hot Chocolate*, *Coffee*, and *Decaf Coffee*.

"You think there's enough choices?" Drew snickers, reading the labels. "Which blend are you going for?"

"Mr. Mynt's. I'm curious if it'll taste minty," I joke. "What about you?"

"Same here." He sets a mug under the spout and fills it. "I'll take care of these. You're on cookie duty."

I salute him. "Yes, sir."

"Whipped cream?" he asks, already reaching for the can.

"Yes. Make it as tall as possible."

"On it." He starts building a whipped-cream mountain.

I head over to the cookie trays, which are stacked with gingerbread men, frosted sugar cookies shaped like trees and snowflakes, and little shortbread stars. I fill a plate with some of everything and glance back at Drew.

Santa's elves are working overtime inside my chest, pounding their hammers against my ribs. Drew is still at the cocoa station, looking adorable. His reindeer antlers sit a little crooked, his brow is furrowed in concentration, and his tongue is poking slightly out of the corner of his mouth as he carefully arranges the peppermint bark shavings. I wish I could sneak out my phone to capture the moment. But I'll settle for a mental snapshot.

I make my way back toward him, balancing a cookie plate in each hand. "How's it going, barista?"

He steps back from the cocoa bar with an exaggerated flourish. "Feast your eyes on these masterpieces."

The whipped cream is piled high and topped with shavings, two mini marshmallows, and, for reasons I don't question, a single red M&M.

"The presentation is a ten out of ten," I say, exchanging a plate for a cup. "But I'm deducting points for the lack of a peppermint stir stick."

He gasps. "I knew I forgot something. Amateur mistake."

"I'll let it slide this time," I say, fighting a smile.

Drew chuckles and nudges me gently toward the lounge seating area, where more guests are filtering in, gathering around the fireplace. A soft instrumental version of "Have Yourself a Merry Little Christmas" plays in the background, blending with the pop and crackle of the fire. We settle onto a pair of oversized floor pillows, close enough that our shoulders brush.

"This is cozy," Drew murmurs, lifting his cup toward mine. "To friendship," he declares with a crooked grin.

"To friendship," I echo, though the words are hollow. We clink our mugs and take a sip. Warmth spreads through me. There's a hint of peppermint and something else unexpectedly sweet. Raspberry? I lick my lips and smile. "It's good."

Drew nods in agreement, eyes still on his cup. "Better than I expected."

The lights dim slightly, and the storyteller begins. "It was the coldest winter the North Pole had ever seen . . ."

I try to focus on the story, but I'm only half listening. The rest of my attention is on the man beside me. I know we said this arrangement was just for fun, but I wish it would turn into something more. I'm playing a dangerous game with my heart.

Chapter Twelve

DREW

After enjoying the story hour, Chloe and I end up walking through the outdoor light trail that wraps around the edge of the resort grounds. The twinkling bulbs cast a soft glow over the frosted trees. She keeps her hands tucked into the sleeves of her green sweater dress.

"You're shivering," I say, stepping a little closer. "Do you want to borrow my sweater?"

She raises an eyebrow. "Do you have anything on under that?"

"Just a T-shirt," I admit.

She shakes her head with a small smile. "Then no way. I'm not risking you getting hypothermia for my sake."

I wouldn't mind being freezing if it meant she saw me as a hero. But she'll probably argue with me if I insist. Still, I'm not giving up. "All right, then how about this . . . May I wrap my arm around you instead?"

She hesitates. "I guess so," she says softly.

I feel a quiet victory swell inside me. This is the opening I've been waiting for. An excuse to be close. I gently slip my left arm around her and pull her in close. The warmth of her body seeps into mine. We walk slowly together, the crunch of snow beneath our feet.

The path winds past candy-cane archways and glowing snowflakes suspended in the trees. Strings of warm bulbs crisscross overhead, and every few feet, there's another photo op setup—sleighs, snowmen, giant presents. We stop at one shaped like a gingerbread house.

"I feel like I should've brought a fork and a gallon of frosting," Chloe says, peeking into the candy-cane-framed doorway. Her breath puffs in the cold, and her nose is pink from the chill.

"You're assuming I'd let you have all the candy for yourself," I say.

She grins. "You'd have to catch me first."

"That's a challenge you'd win, hands down. I've seen you glide around the rink. The rules of gravity don't apply to you."

She laughs. That sound's quickly becoming one of my favorite features of hers. As I study her, I notice that her hair glints in the soft lights of the trees, a mix of gold and chestnut. There's no script for this moment. Just the steady rhythm of our footsteps crunching in the snow.

I tilt my head toward her. My pulse starts to race. "Chloe," I whisper. I stop walking and reach up, brushing a strand of hair away from her face. My fingers graze her cheek, and there's the slightest tremble beneath my touch. Whether it's the cold or something else, I'm not sure.

She doesn't pull back. "I've wanted to tell you for a long time," I say, my voice low. "I've always thought you're beautiful."

She breathes in, her lips parting slightly. Her eyes find mine. They're wide and bright, illuminated by the glow of twinkling lights overhead. I feel more connected to her than I ever have before. There's an invisible thread, slowly pulling us together.

I lean in, slow enough to give her a chance to stop me. But she doesn't. Her breath catches. Our foreheads touch for the briefest moment. Then our lips meet.

Our kiss is soft. Tentative. Like we're testing the waters of something we've both secretly wanted but have been too afraid to ask for. Her lips are warm despite the cold, and I taste a hint of peach from her lip gloss. My heart pounds in my chest. I can't quite believe this is real. There's nothing pretend about this.

"Oh. My. Gosh!"

We break apart like guilty teenagers.

Emma's hands fly to her mouth, eyes wide with glee. "I knew it was only a matter of time before you got together." She claps her hands together. "I'm so happy right now! My best friend and my brother are an item!" My sister launches forward, throwing her arms around both of us in a tackle hug. "This is the best Christmas gift ever!"

I groan. "Emma—"

"Nope. Don't even try to deny it," she cuts in, releasing us. "You guys look like you've got mistletoe growing out of your heads."

Chloe covers her face with her hands.

Emma narrows her eyes like a bloodhound on a scent. "When did you make it official?"

I glance at Chloe, unsure of what to say. Her lips are slightly parted, her cheeks flushed, and I can't tell if she's more shocked or embarrassed. Maybe both. Probably both.

Another beat of silence passes.

"It literally just happened," Chloe finally says.

"Wait, did I just interrupt your first kiss?"

We both nod.

"I feel awful. I was just heading to the parking lot and then I saw you two all cozy under the lights, and I thought . . . well, I didn't think. Obviously. Should I go? I can disappear. Pretend I was never here."

Before I can say a word, Chloe says, "Actually, I should get going." Her voice is soft. "I promised I'd check in with the Mynt to Make a Difference coordinator about tomorrow's events."

Emma frowns, clearly sensing something's off. "Oh."

"I'll catch up with you guys later, okay?" Chloe flashes a quick wave. She doesn't meet my gaze as she disappears quickly down the trail, leaving behind a small trail of footprints on the snow-covered path.

I'm left staring after her fleeing form, my lips still tingling from the kiss.

Emma shifts beside me. "Okaaay. What just happened?"

I drag a hand through my hair. "Nothing."

"That wasn't nothing," she says, her voice rising an octave. "That was *something*. With a capital S. Not to mention the sparks of tension between you two! Are you seriously going to pretend I imagined that?"

I exhale. "No. Yes. I don't know."

"I've never seen you so flustered." Emma studies me. "You really like her, don't you?"

"Yeah. I do." I pause. "C'mon, I'll walk with you to your car."

She falls into step beside me. The air is cold and smells faintly of pine needles and mud. "I didn't mean to interrupt you guys. If I'd known, I would've stayed hidden behind the gingerbread house."

"It's okay," I say, though the words feel empty. It's not her fault.

"But it was your *first kiss*. You can't redo a first kiss!"

"Maybe not," I murmur, stuffing my hands into my pockets. "But maybe there'll be another chance."

We reach the edge of the lot. Emma pauses. "So . . . what are you going to do?"

"About?"

"The kiss," she says earnestly.

I stare up at the sky for a second. The stars are beginning to peek out through the clouds. "I don't know. Except I don't want to mess up whatever is going on between Chloe and me," I admit.

"You won't," Emma says, suddenly serious.

I glance over. "How do you know?"

"Because I've seen how you guys look at one another. Everything is gonna work out." She bumps my arm. "Also, have you thought about what you want to get her for Christmas?"

"A little." I pull out my phone and open the internet browser to the page I have bookmarked. It's a webstore that sells custom skate blades. "I was thinking maybe a pair of these. I want to get Chloe something meaningful that she'll use."

Emma snorts. "There's nothing more romantic than a weapon for her feet."

"Emma . . ." I groan.

"I'm just telling you the truth."

I ignore her. "I thought maybe I could pick up a pair and get them engraved with something like her initials or something fun like, 'toe pick.'"

"You do *not* put 'toe pick' on there."

"Why not?"

"You need to watch *The Cutting Edge*."

"Never heard of it."

"The DVD is on my bookshelf. It's one of Chloe's all-time favorite movies."

That gets my attention. I know what I'll be doing tonight.

Emma reaches for my phone. "Mind if I browse?"

"Knock yourself out."

She scrolls for a few seconds. "These come in different sizes and specs . . ." she mutters.

"I know. I was trying to come up with a way to casually ask her about her current blades, but I haven't gotten the chance yet."

Emma glances up at me. "Did you even check how much these cost?"

"No." I shake my head.

She whistles low. "Okay, well the basic ones start at around three hundred bucks. But for someone at Chloe's level? You're looking more at seven or eight hundred dollars."

I wince. "That's way out of my budget."

She nods, handing me back my phone. "What about something similar like an ice-skate necklace?"

I blink a few times. "Why didn't I think of that? That's perfect. I could still get it engraved too."

"There we go." She straightens, smug. "And since I'm the best sister ever, I'll go to the mall and find it for you."

"Thanks, but I'd rather do it my—"

She holds up her hand. "No offense," she says, arching a brow, "but it's a few days before Christmas. You hate when the mall is crowded during normal times of year. How do you think it's gonna be now? In a mall full of frantic shoppers?"

"Busy."

"Uh-huh. You'll be eaten alive if you go."

"And you won't?"

"Uh, no. I thrive in chaos." She grins. "Trust me. I'm a concierge extraordinaire. If I can organize a wedding proposal, three anniversary surprises, and a llama-themed vow renewal in the same weekend, I can shop 'til I drop and help my brother win over one skater girl."

As much as I hate to inflate her already massive ego, this *is* Emma's wheelhouse. And I'm officially out of my depth. "Fine. But you better call me the second you find something. I want to pick it out."

"Deal." She holds out her hand. "Credit card?"

I dig out my wallet. "Try to stay under a hundred bucks. Mom and Dad don't pay me much."

"Love is priceless," she says with a grin, snatching the card. "But I'll stay within your sad little budget."

She turns toward her car, ponytail swaying, already pulling up the mall directory on her phone. I stand there for a moment, surrounded by snow and string lights, wondering how I fell so hard, so fast, for the one girl I never planned to fall for.

A little later, my phone buzzes and I see *Incoming Video Call: Emma*. I swipe to accept the call. "Hey—"

The camera shakes violently before focusing on a crowded jewelry store. "Santa Baby" blares in the background, and Emma's breath is coming in short, exaggerated puffs. "I'm in," she says dramatically. "I had to circle the parking lot for an hour to get parked. But I made it."

"You sound like you've just participated in a polar plunge."

Emma flips the camera to show me the mob of shoppers pushing past her. "It's *war*, Drew. There was an actual skirmish over a weighted blanket and peppermint lip gloss."

I could not be more grateful Emma's at the mall and not me. "You're ridiculous."

"You say that now, but wait until you see this."

The camera shifts again. This time, she's zooming in on a delicate silver necklace, shaped like an ice skate. It's exactly what I had in mind. My heart starts playing a drum solo. "That's it."

"I thought so," she says smugly. "It's understated, but still says, 'I pay attention to what you love, and I am a thoughtful human being.'"

"Did you check if it can be engraved?"

"I did. The woman behind the counter said she can have it ready in an hour. What do you want it to say?" Emma gives me a flat look. "I swear, if you ruin this with a *Cutting Edge* joke, I will buy her novelty socks instead."

I'd thought long and hard about this. Chloe needs to know that she isn't alone. Emma and I will always be there for her. I think back to the drive the three of us took five years ago.

We'd just crossed the Colorado state line, and it wouldn't be long before we hit the turnoff to the farm. Chloe and I had been swapping questions for a couple hours, getting to know each other and all I kept thinking was—Emma couldn't have picked a better person to call her best friend.

"Is it hard to be alone on the ice all the time?" I asked. "Do you ever wish you had a partner?"

Chloe glanced over at me, then back out the window.

"When I was younger, I thought pairs or ice dance might be fun. But my parents didn't approve. Singles is what gets the most attention at the Olympics, not the other disciplines." She fiddled with the hem of her sweater. "As for being alone . . . I've gotten used to it. On and off the ice."

As I opened my mouth to ask what she meant, Emma woke up, yawned, and shouted from the back seat, "Hey, bro, I'm starving. Can we stop for some breakfast soon?"

"Yeah, sure."

It wasn't until Emma's graduation that I finally put the pieces together and saw it for what it was. The way her family treated her. How small they made her feel. And now, more than ever, I just want to do the opposite.

"Have them put 'In your corner. Always.'"

Emma's eyes widen. "Sometimes you still manage to surprise me, bro."

I select a font, and she promises she'll call me again when it's ready to make sure everything looks perfect. As I hang up, I wonder if there's a few more surprises I can plan for Chloe to make this Christmas *really* stand out for her. She deserves it.

Chapter Thirteen

CHLOE

I sit on the edge of my bed. My hands are still trembling from the cold. My coat is in a puddle on the floor. My antlers and bulb necklace lie tangled on the nightstand. I haven't even taken my boots off. What just happened? The question loops through my brain like a broken music box that won't shut off.

Hanging out with Drew was supposed to be a safe way to live out one of the dreams I'd been nursing since I met the man. The stakes were low because I knew he wasn't interested in me. But somewhere between our skating lesson, cocoa in the lounge, and that quiet walk under the lights, things change. I can't stop thinking about the way his hands felt on my back, how his eyes found mine, and the soft way he told me I was beautiful right before we kissed, and my brain short-circuited.

I press my hands to my cheeks. They're still warm and probably as red as Rudolph's nose. Was that real? Did he feel it too?

I want to believe the answer is yes. That I didn't

imagine any of it. But then Emma showed up. And now I can't stop wondering what would've happened next.

Part of me wants to march back downstairs, find Drew, and ask him point-blank what the kiss meant to him. But I won't. Because I'm not sure I'm ready to hear the answer. That's probably why I ran away like a coward.

I kick off my boots, tug my sweater dress over my head, and swap it for my softest snowflake pajamas. Then I climb under the covers and pull the blanket over my head, like that might shield me from the confusion swirling around in my chest.

My phone buzzes against the nightstand just as I'm burrowing deeper under the covers, still pretending last night ended with Drew confessing he's always loved me instead of me panicking and bolting. I groan and crack one eye open. A text from Emma lights up the screen.

Emma: Breakfast?

I stare at the message, weighing my options. I could hide under these blankets until it's time to head to the rink for lessons at ten. But avoiding Emma will only make things worse.

Chloe: What time?

Emma: Now?

I snort. Of course she's already down in the lobby.

Chloe: Be down in ten.

Emma: Mm-kay. Meet me at the cafe. I just ordered you a peppermint mocha. Omelet to go with it?

Chloe: You know me. *Winking emoji*

With a sigh, I throw off the covers and tug on a pair of Mynt Athletic leggings, a pine-green tank top, and a soft resort hoodie. My hair's a mess, but I manage to twist it into a loose braid before pulling on my boots and heading downstairs.

The café smells like cinnamon and roasted coffee beans. The quiet clink of spoons against ceramic mugs feels way too chipper for seven a.m. Emma's already claimed a corner table, waving me over like she's been here for a few hours.

"You're the best," I mumble, sliding into the seat across from her and wrapping my hands around the peppermint mocha. I take a long sip, letting the chocolate and crushed peppermint melt on my tongue. "I didn't realize how badly I needed this."

"Did you get any sleep? Because you look like you were visited by the ghosts of Christmas past, present, and future," she says gently, not teasing for once.

"Not much," I mutter.

A beat of silence stretches between us while we sip our drinks. Then Emma says softly, "I wanted to apologize again. For last night. I still feel awful."

A server arrives with two omelets. The plates are loaded with potatoes, spinach, peppers, and chicken. "It's fine, Em," I murmur, picking up the salsa bottle and dumping some on top of the chicken.

Emma leans forward, brow raised. "It's not. I know you've been pining after my brother since Fresno. I should've realized you two were having your 'ah-ha' moment. If someone crashed my big moment, I'd be furious."

I freeze, fork halfway to my mouth. "I didn't realize it was that obvious," I murmur.

Emma smiles. "You looked like a kid on Christmas morning. And so did he." She pauses. "For what it's worth, Drew hasn't looked that happy since before he moved to LA."

I blink at her, caught off guard by the weight of her words. Was he really happy last night? "Are you being serious?" I ask carefully.

"Yes." Emma nods as she slices into her omelet. "He's been mopey for the last couple months." She pauses, glancing up at me. "But last night. . .the way he looked at you, Chloe? I don't think he's ever looked at anyone like that."

I drop my gaze to my plate and nudge a piece of egg around with my fork. Part of me wants to believe every word she's saying. That maybe this isn't all one-sided. But there's still an alarm blaring in my mind screaming "Caution, caution."

"I don't know what to think," I say finally, my voice low. "It felt real, but I've never been on Drew's radar like that before."

Emma tilts her head. "Are you sure about that?"

I look up, startled.

"Maybe he didn't make it obvious, but he's always tuned in whenever your name has come up in conversation. And I don't think it was just because you were my friend." She stirs her coffee slowly. "I always thought it might be more than that. And last night confirmed it for me."

I stare at her, the fork slipping from my fingers and clinking softly against the plate. "He's never said anything," I manage.

Emma lifts one shoulder. "Drew's always been weird about sharing any of his feelings with me. It's not something brothers usually discuss with their younger sisters."

My stomach knots tighter. "He said I looked beautiful," I murmur, more to myself than to her.

Emma pauses mid-sip and gives me a puzzled look.

I look away, focusing on my half-eaten omelet and poking at the remaining salsa with my fork. I've never been more tempted to break down and tell her everything. Emma's been my best friend since freshman year. We've never kept things from one another. Not my skating struggles or even her ill-advised attempt to flirt with my hot calculus TA by crashing his office hours despite not even being in the class.

But this? This feels different. Because what's happening with Drew, I want to hold on to for a little while longer before the rest of the world gets a say. So I keep it to myself. Just a little longer. Until I figure out where this is really going. I force a small smile and push my plate aside. "I think I need to get out on the ice for a bit. Clear my head."

Emma's features soften. "You okay?"

"I will be," I say, managing a small smile.

She doesn't press. And I'm grateful for that. There are so many questions about Drew swirling around in my head. Can I trust him? Nick wasn't the only guy who has ever let me down. The same thing happened at the Nationals banquet two years ago.

I finished fourth and was awarded the pewter medal. Most skaters wouldn't be too happy about it, but I was thrilled. It was still a podium finish. And that was my best result to date.

"Hey, Chloe, congrats," Adam, a bronze medalist in ice dance, said as we lined up backstage for the final bow of the exhibition gala performance.

"Thank you."

"Are you going to the closing banquet with anyone?"

I hesitated. I usually skipped those things. It was awkward to be alone. My coaches were never able to go, and it wasn't like I had my family here to support me. This time, however, something in me wavered. "I was on the fence," I admitted.

"Oh," he said, running a hand through his hair. "I was going to ask if you wanted to be my date."

My throat tightened. A date? I hadn't been on one since Nick. The word alone sent a ripple of nerves through me. Did I say yes? Make up an excuse? I hated how hard it was to tell what the right answer was when my anxiety kicked in.

Still, maybe it was time I put myself out there. Adam didn't seem like the type who'd bail. "Sure," I said, trying to keep my voice steady.

"Awesome. It starts at seven. Do you want me to swing by your room at six forty-five?"

Heat seared my cheeks. "I'm not staying at the official hotel. So it'll have to be the lobby."

"Oh, OK. That works."

At times like these, I wished my pride would allow me to let my parents pay for my travel and accommodations. They wouldn't bat an eyelash at the expense. It would've been so much easier to be where everyone else was staying. But then I remembered that help from them always came with strings. I was better off on my own.

The venue was a twenty-minute walk from my motel. It was just after five. I should have just enough time to make a pit stop at Zara and find something to wear, since I didn't bring a formal dress with me.

When I got there, the pickings were slim, but I managed to find a simple black dress that would do the job. Back at the motel, I showered, applied a light layer of makeup, and headed out the door in record time. I sent Adam a text.

Chloe: On my way. See you soon.

During the walk to the hotel, my heart was racing. I smoothed my hands down the skirt of my new dress for the tenth time, willing myself not to overthink things. This didn't have to mean anything big.

It was just a banquet, just one evening. Still, a tiny flicker of hope stirred in my chest. Could Adam be interested in me? Was there a sliver of a chance that tonight's date could turn into something more?

I arrived in the lobby at six-forty. There was no sign of Adam. It was fine. I was early. He did say six forty-five. I found a seat near the fireplace and crossed my ankles, watching the elevator with quiet anticipation. Ten minutes went by. Then twenty. The flicker of hope started to dim. I sent him another message.

Chloe: Just checking in. I'm in the lobby. Are you on your way down?

I hit Send and glanced toward the front desk, half-expecting to see him coming around the corner. Nothing.

Another thirty minutes slipped by before my phone finally buzzed.

> Adam: Hey, sorry. I'm on my way to the airport. They issued a severe storm warning for Detroit. I didn't want to get stuck. If I didn't leave now, I might be stuck for three or four days. There wasn't enough time to text you.

I stared at the message, the words blurring for a second. There was time. Even a one-line text would've done the job. Especially if he was already in a car, supposedly heading to the airport. He just didn't bother. I wished he'd said what we both knew was true—he forgot about me. Or worse, changed his mind.

> Chloe: No harm done. Have a safe flight.

I hit Send, but my fingers felt numb. I should've known better. I always did this—started to believe that someone might actually want to show up for me.

A group of male skaters walked by laughing in formal wear, and suddenly, I felt like a spectator in someone else's evening. I slipped out quietly through the revolving doors before anyone I knew could spot me, stepping into the cold night and pretending I wasn't disappointed.

I never heard from him again. The only upside to the whole night was the early warning about the storm. I managed to catch a flight out before it hit.

That trip home was quiet. I spent most of the flight staring out the window, replaying every second of that night like it was somehow my fault. I kept wondering if I expected too much from people. If maybe I was the kind of person who was easy to forget. It really got me thinking about the type of skater I was.

Three weeks passed, and I couldn't shake the fog. It

wasn't just about Adam. It was about my nonexistent coach too. I was tired of being overlooked. To Coach Jon, I was a skater past her prime.

I'd probably never do better than fourth place. The solid alternate for the World and Olympic teams. His attention always went to his fifteen- and sixteen-year-old jumping beans, who were working on multiple triple-triples and even a triple Axel. I needed a fresh start. So I took my destiny into my own hands and decided to make a call, despite feeling some nerves.

"Hello?" The man had answered right away, his voice warm and marked with a soft Spanish accent.

"Hi, Mr. Alvarez? This is Chloe Reynolds. I don't know if you remember me—we met during practice at Nationals. My coach had to leave early, and you helped me with my triple loop."

"Hola, Chloe. Please, call me Fernando. And sí, I remember you." He chuckled. "How can I help you?"

Just hearing his voice put me at ease. Everything inside me said I was doing the right thing. "I was wondering if you're accepting new students. I've decided to part ways with my coach, Jon Harper."

"Sí. Especially someone with as much natural talent as you. There's one catch though . . ."

"Okay," I said cautiously.

"You wouldn't just be getting me as a coach. You'd be getting Charlie Welch and Frankie Tomlinson too. We work as a team."

I let out a laugh. "That actually sounds amazing."

Charlie Welch and Frankie Tomlinson? That was too good to be true! They were the Olympic champions in pairs. I couldn't believe I'd get to be on the same ice as them, let alone be coached by them.

"I'm glad to hear it. Would you be willing to come to Sequoia Valley for a trial period?"

"Yes, please."

"When would you like to start?"

"As soon as I can."

I started training with Charlie, Frankie, and Fernando. We clicked right away. They're not just coaches. They're my friends too. Charlie knows exactly how to push me without breaking me. Fernando and Frankie have this way of reminding me that skating should still be joyful, even when it's hard. And because of them, I fell in love with the sport again. And more than that—they've helped me start believing in myself again too.

By the time I make it to the rink an hour later, the sun's peeking through the clouds, casting a faint golden glow over the snow-dusted trees. I lace up my skates and tug my gloves on tighter. The air is sharp and cold, stinging my cheeks the moment I step onto the ice.

The resort staff has just resurfaced it, and the surface gleams like crystal. It's untouched and perfect. I take a breath and push off, my blades whispering across the glassy surface. The weight in my chest starts to lift. This is my happy place.

I circle the rink once, warming up with crossovers and power pulls. Then I head to the center of the ice and fall into the opening choreography of my short program.

There's no music playing over the speakers, but I don't need it. I hear every note in my head. Every beat. Each movement is stitched into my muscle memory. I launch into my triple flip-triple toe, land it cleanly, and glide into an Ina Bauer. The movements aren't just routine right now —they're a release.

When I finally come to the ending pose, I'm breathless. My pulse drums in my ears, but my head feels clearer than it has since I arrived.

I sink down onto the ice for a moment. My muscles are still trembling from all the energy I pushed out. I've spent so long being quiet about what I wanted. But that's about to end. I'm tired of staying silent. I want Drew. It's time to tell him the truth about how I've always felt about him.

Every time I closed my eyes last night, all I could see was Chloe walking away. I should've gone after her. Instead, I let her leave, and now I think I've blown it. I just stood there as frozen as a snowman. The truth's been sitting in my chest for years, and I still couldn't get the words out. I just don't know how. Yet.

After tossing and turning all night, around three a.m., I decided to just get up. I pulled on my heavy parka, rummaged through the basement until I found a dusty plastic bin labeled *Holiday Aquascaping Stuff*, and drove to the resort. Luckily, it's a lot like Vegas. The work doesn't stop just because it's night. Nobody batted an eyelash when I showed up and started lugging the box full of decorations to the tank area.

Right now, it's about eight a.m. A couple of maintenance workers pause nearby, watching as I step back and examine the tank's transformation. The new aquatic plants sway gently in the current, anchored in carefully arranged red and green sand and stones. I've added a few resin ornaments in red, gold, and icy-blue. They're safe for the fish, but festive enough to look like tiny underwater ornaments. My favorite details, though, are the miniature sleigh and Santa nestled behind a piece of driftwood. It's subtle, but it makes the whole thing feel like Christmas.

I used to decorate my own tanks like this every December, before I moved to LA. I didn't realize how much I'd missed it until now. The water's already starting to clear, and the fish—neon tetras, a couple gold barbs, and two little Cory catfish—dart in and out of the rock tunnels, checking out the new additions.

"That's pretty awesome," a voice says behind me.

I turn to find Robert, Emma's coworker, standing beside me with a clipboard in one hand and a steaming cup of coffee in the other.

"Thanks," I say, brushing my damp hands on a towel draped over my shoulder. "Figured the fish deserved some holiday cheer too."

Robert chuckles and heads off, leaving me alone with the soft hum of the filter. I crouch back down and continue to watch as the fish weave through the plants and decorations. "If only figuring out what to say to Chloe were as easy as decorating the tank," I mutter under my breath.

Footsteps echo on the tile behind me, followed by the jingle of a key-card lanyard. I glance over my shoulder just as Mr. Mynt stops a few feet away. He's wearing black pants, a red suit jacket, a green tie with tiny peppermints, and a Santa hat. I have to hand it to him. He knows how to dress.

"Good morning, Mr. Mynt."

"Good morning." He crosses his arms and studies the tank.

I hold my breath.

"This is *quite* an improvement," he says suddenly. "I'd forgotten we had an aquarium over here."

I rise, brushing some stray gravel from my jeans. "Thanks."

He lifts an eyebrow, clearly impressed. "And I take it this setup is all you?"

"Guilty as charged," I say, rubbing the back of my neck. "The rest of the resort was decked out, and I figured the fish deserved the same courtesy."

Mr. Mynt nods slowly. He leans even closer, smiling as his eyes find the sleigh. "You've got an eye for detail." He turns his head my direction. "You're a Sullivan, right? Bill and Angie's son?"

I nod. "Yes, sir."

"Makes sense." He chuckles. "It looks like the creative streak runs in the family." He strokes his chin thoughtfully. "I don't suppose you'd be interested in doing another one like this? There's a ten-foot-long tank sitting in the storage room. I was just thinking something like this would be the perfect addition to the decor for the Merry Mynt Ball on the twenty-third."

It takes me a second to process what he's asking. "You want me to design and install a tank for the event?"

"If you can have it set up by the morning of the twenty-third," he confirms. "You'd have an unlimited budget and access to whatever materials you need. Think you're up for it?"

My heart jumps. That's two days from now. A ten-foot tank would be pushing two hundred gallons minimum. My mind starts racing. I'd need to clean everything, test and install the filtration system and lighting, place the designs, then stock it.

If I don't sleep, it's doable, but there's no way I can fully cycle a tank of that size so quickly if I want to be able to safely introduce the fish. Letting the nitrogen levels stabilize in the tank normally takes six to eight weeks.

"I can't fully cycle the tank by then," I admit, already troubleshooting in my head. "But if it's just for display during the ball, I can pre-seed the filters using the media from another tank and keep the fish in there for the short-term."

"I have no idea of what any of that means, but if it's temporary, that's fine," Mr. Mynt says, nodding. "We just need it to look good for the event. After that, you can make whatever adjustments you think are necessary so we can make it a more permanent feature of the ballroom."

I hesitate for only a second longer, but I already know the answer. "In that case, I'd love to." My hands are practically itching to sketch out ideas already. I see shimmering white gravel, clusters of red and gold plants, a bubble wand shaped like a candy cane, and maybe even a small model of the resort. That is if I can 3-D print or sculpt one quick enough.

"Excellent. I'll have someone wheel the tank and all the equipment that goes with it to the ballroom this afternoon. Bill whatever you need to the resort. Your sister should have the account information."

I glance back at the holiday tank I just finished. And for the first time in months, I feel excited about having a project to work on. "It's been a long time since I've done anything like this," I admit.

"I'm sure it'll turn out fantastic." Mr. Mynt smiles. "I'm always looking for ways to add unique touches to the resort for our guests. Perhaps after the holidays, we could discuss a few more collaborations I'd like to do."

I blink, caught off guard. "You want me to design more tanks?"

"Absolutely. Consider this a trial run." He extends a hand. "What was your name again?"

"I'm Drew," I say, still a little stunned.

"Well, Drew, it's early days, but I have a good feeling about you." He winks. "Welcome to the Mynt family."

As he walks away, I just stand there, wondering if I'd heard him right. I came home trying to figure out what was next. It never crossed my mind that designing tanks *professionally* could actually be part of that answer. I grin widely. If I do this right and Mr. Mynt commissions me for more tanks, I could use my work here to build a portfolio. Could this be something I do full-time in the future?

Excitement buzzes through me. I pull out my phone, swipe open the notes app, and start sketching ideas. I can already picture the glow of blue LEDs, icy gravel, and delicate ornaments swirling like snow beneath the water's surface. My pulse is thrumming with possibility.

"Wow," Emma says, joining me as I'm packing up the last of my supplies. She hands me a cup of coffee and a cinnamon twist in a paper bag.

It's uncanny how she's always ready with exactly what I need. "How did you know I haven't had breakfast yet?"

"I can anticipate the needs of most of our resort guests. Call it the concierge sixth sense."

I snort and take a massive bite of the cinnamon twist, letting the sugar and pastry calm the nervous churning in my stomach.

"And also," she adds, "I saw you working over here like a madman when I walked in to meet Chloe for breakfast."

My jaw pauses mid-chew. I glance sideways. "How is she?" I try to make it sound casual, but the question still comes out rough.

Emma's expression softens. "She's okay. She has a lot on her mind and just needs some time to sort through her feelings and clear her head."

I nod, but my stomach twists. That's code for not interested in me, isn't it?

"She's at the rink," Emma says.

I want to ask more details. Was she upset? Did she talk about me? But I clamp down on it. I already feel like I'm the reason she needed space in the first place.

Emma reaches into her coat pocket and pulls out my credit card. "By the way, here."

I take it. "You're returning this without a receipt? That's a bad sign," I deadpan.

"Relax." She digs into her tote bag and hands me a small, wrapped box. "I spent $99.87. Thirteen cents under budget. You're welcome."

I look down at the box in my hand. The wrapping is neat. It has green paper, silver ribbon, and a tiny glittery snowflake charm attached to the bow. I slide it into my coat pocket. I hope trusting my sister was the right thing to do. "When do I give it to her?"

"When the timing's right. You'll just know."

"You're impossible," I mutter.

"And yet, you still gave me your credit card." She grins.

We start walking toward the front lobby doors. Outside, snow has started falling again, dusting the walkway. Emma pauses in the doorway and turns to me, her expression unusually serious. "What are you doing following me?"

I blink. "What?"

"You heard me. I told you where to find Chloe."

"I thought you said she needed to think?" To me, that means being alone. Unless my sister knows something I don't.

"She does. But you should still go talk to her." Emma's tone shifts, becoming softer. "If you're scared this thing between you is one-sided, you're wrong. And if you mess it up by hesitating too long . . . well, I'll be forced to get involved."

I raise an eyebrow. "Weren't you already involved?"

"Exactly." She gives me a pointed look, then heads back to the concierge desk.

I stand there for a second, holding the warm coffee in one hand, the gift tucked into my pocket. Chloe is just a short walk away. Every part of me is screaming to go to her. But then I remember the look on her face when she walked away. She was overwhelmed. Like me. If I'm serious about this thing we have going between us, I need to respect her and give her some space.

So instead of heading for the rink, I find a bench just outside the main building, brush it off, and sit. I can't see Chloe or the ice from here, but I know she's out there. And if she does happen to head this way, I'll be waiting for her.

In the meantime, I take a sip of my coffee and finish the cinnamon twist. I pull out my phone and open my notes app again to keep brainstorming about Mr. Mynt's tank.

Chapter Fifteen

CHLOE

By the time I finish teaching lessons today, leave the rink, and tug off my skates, the storm inside my chest has finally settled. I don't have all the answers, but the fog has lifted just enough for me to see where I want to go next. I'm not pretending anymore with my feelings. Now, I just have to figure out what to say to Drew. But first, I need to get through the rest of today.

The afternoon sun filters weakly through a blanket of gray clouds as I step into the room near the fireside lounge. Long folding tables line the space. Each one contains stacks of bins with craft supplies for the ornament-decorating event. There are wooden sticks, glitter glue, pipe cleaners, buttons, yarn, and lots of sequins. The room smells like popcorn, cinnamon, and glue.

A volunteer in a red "Mynt to Make a Difference" sweatshirt waves me over. "Hey there, are you one of the athletes checking in?"

"Yes, I'm Chloe," I say, offering a smile.

She scans the list and beams. "Perfect timing. We've got about twenty people signed up today, and they're already trickling in. I hope you don't mind going home covered in glitter."

"I'll take my chances." I laugh as I slide into a seat at the nearest table.

There are two other athletes here. I recognize Michelle, the golfer from the other day, and one of the guys I met at the rink, Robert the speedskater. I wave to both of them. So far, getting to know the other athletes during lunch hasn't been too bad. They've been relatively down-to-earth. I still feel like a fish out of water, but a lot better than I did a few days ago.

Across from me, a gap-toothed girl with sparkly barrettes in her braids is enthusiastically gluing rhinestones to a felt Christmas tree. "Hi," I say, "I'm Chloe."

"I'm Sofie." She proudly holds up her work like it belongs in a museum.

"You're doing an amazing job." I help her attach a gold ribbon to the top of her tree, and the way her whole face lights up warms my heart. Her joy is why I'm here at the resort. Not just to skate or fulfill my obligations to Mr. Mynt's company, but to give back and be a part of something that matters.

However, despite trying to focus on helping Sofie glue sequins and tie ribbons, part of my mind keeps drifting back to Drew. I can't get that kiss out of my head. His voice was so soft and tender. His fingers gently brushed across my cheeks. And when his lips met mine, it was like the fireworks show at Disneyland.

You turn up early to find a good spot. The anticipation builds and you wait for it to begin. Then finally, when the music starts, it sends chills through your bones, and the whole thing culminates in an explosion of color. That's exactly how I felt last night. His kiss was everything

I'd been waiting for and more. I just wish it had lasted longer.

I finish tying a bow onto another ornament and exhale slowly. When the hour is up, I brush stray glitter off my sweater, thank the volunteer coordinator, and step back into the hallway.

I need to find Drew. I don't have a speech ready, but I know I have to talk to him. This time, I'm not waiting for something to happen—I'm going after it.

I head for the lobby, my gut insisting he'll be close. When I push open the door to the courtyard, cold air brushes my cheeks, and then I see him.

He's sitting beneath the pergola strung with holly, red ribbon, and twinkling lights. Snow dusts his hair, and there's a furrow between his brows as he types something on his phone. He looks thoughtful and hard at work on something. He also looks exhausted. I hope it's not my fault for keeping him out late. I know he has to get up early to help at the shop.

He glances up from his coffee mid-sip and sees me. For half a second, surprise flickers across his face, followed by a wide smile.

I cross the patio quickly. My nerves flutter like snowflakes caught in a breeze. "Hey," I say.

"Hey," he says, setting his phone aside. "Where did you come from? You're, uh, covered in glitter."

I glance down at my blue sweater and grimace, brushing off the sleeves and bottom. "Ugh, I thought I got it all."

"It's a good look for you." He laughs softly, as he stands. The sound warm and familiar, and it sends my heart racing.

I tuck a strand of hair behind my ear. "I just came from an ornament-decorating event."

"Gotcha." He's still watching me, eyes softer now, like he's seeing something he hadn't noticed before.

Silence fills the space. His hand lifts and his fingertips graze over the edge of my sleeve, brushing away a few stray pieces of glitter. He doesn't pull away. Instead, his fingers trail lightly along my wrist, then stop just shy of my hand. He pulls me closer toward him.

My breath catches. I don't move, and neither does he. Our eyes meet. The snow, the lights, the distant sound of laughter—they all fade into a muffled hush. All I can hear is the rush of my own heartbeat.

He leans in a fraction. So do I. He's right there. My lips part, just slightly, just in case . . . but then he blinks and quickly looks away.

Darn it. I was really, really hoping for . . . well, never mind. It's not going to happen.

Drew clears his throat and glances away, like the moment caught him off guard too. Like he wasn't sure if he imagined it—or if I did. He gestures to where he was sitting on the bench. "Care to join me?"

"Sure." I sit and stare out across the snowy path. It looks so different out here in the daytime.

"What are you working on?" I ask, looking for a way to start the conversation.

"Oh, something for Mr. Mynt. He has an aquarium he wanted designed. And he wants me to do it."

"Drew, that's fantastic." I clap my hands together. "I want to hear all about it!"

"I'm not sure if I can share anything about it yet . . ." He hesitates. "I need to clear it with Mr. Mynt's office first."

I nod in understanding. We sit in silence for another moment. Then I take a deep breath. "I've been thinking about last night," I say at the same time he says, "About last night."

We share a chuckle.

His eyes find mine. "Go ahead. What were you going to say?"

I twist my fingers together inside the sleeves of my sweater, then look down at my lap. "I've *always* liked you, Drew." My voice catches slightly. "More than I probably should. To the point where sometimes it hurt since I knew you'd never notice me." I take a shaky breath and lift my gaze to his, my throat tightening. "But when we kissed last night, it was like a dream. Like someone flipped on the lights in a room I didn't realize I'd been standing in the dark in."

He still doesn't say anything. He watches me with a deep, unreadable look that makes me feel like I'm both coming undone and finally being seen. "Chloe—" he starts.

I interrupt, losing my nerve. "It's okay if you don't feel the same way as me. I just . . . I couldn't keep it in anymore. And if that means you want to end our friendship, I . . . I'll understand."

"Chloe." He shifts on the bench. He places his hand under my chin and lifts it gently, his eyes searching mine. "Can I say something now?"

I nod, unable to speak around the knot in my throat.

"I've never seen you as *just* Emma's friend," he says, his voice quieter now. "Not even close." He takes a deep breath. "You've always been one of the most beautiful, thoughtful people I've ever known. And the most grounded. Honestly, that scared me a little."

I blink, caught off guard by the rawness in his voice. He releases my chin.

"I always thought you were way out of my league," he admits.

I tilt my head to the side and blink in disbelief. "You thought I was out of your league?"

He gives a small, sheepish smile. "I was the guy who took the first job he got and hoped it would be enough. You're the woman who's always had this drive and determination and knows exactly what she wants."

I almost laugh because if that were true, I would've gone for him four years ago, not waited this long!

He exhales, a puff of breath curling in the crisp air. "I think that's part of why I never said anything. Not because I didn't notice you, Chloe, but because I thought you'd shoot me down."

My chest tightens. Every word he says feels like it's peeling back a layer of bubble wrap I've carefully kept over my heart.

He shakes his head, almost like he still can't believe this is happening. "But last night . . . I felt something between us change. And I haven't been able to stop thinking about you. About *us*."

His hand finds mine. The contact sends a warm current up my arm. "I want to take a chance and see where this thing between us goes," he says.

Suddenly there's no chatter, no laughter from the lounge, or wind blowing through the pergola. It's only the two of us.

I lick my lips. There are a dozen snowflakes caught in a gust fluttering inside my stomach. Drew's gaze dips to my mouth, then slowly lifts again. His eyes lock onto mine with an intensity that sends another shiver down my spine. He's not just looking at me. He's seeing me—all of me. And for once, I don't want to look away.

There's no formal invitation. Just a magnetic pull between us, louder than any words urging us together. Time slows as we lean in toward one another. Our lips meet in a soft, gentle kiss. He tastes like peppermint and cinnamon.

His hand slides up to cup my cheek, his thumb sweeping gently across my skin, and I melt into him. My fingers find the front of his jacket, clutching it lightly to anchor myself, because I swear the ground beneath me doesn't feel steady anymore.

It's not a dramatic kiss. There are no fireworks. But it's something better. It's steady, warm, and deep, like coming home after a long, cold day and wrapping yourself up in a plush, heated blanket.

When we finally pull back, our foreheads rest together, and neither of us says anything. We're both breathing hard.

A wide smile stretches across my lips. "Having you by my side is the best Christmas gift I could've asked for," I murmur.

Drew leans back just enough to reach into his jacket pocket. "Speaking of gifts, I almost forgot . . ." He pulls out a small box wrapped in green paper and silver ribbon and hands it to me, a little sheepish. "This is for you."

The tag reads,

To Chloe, from Drew (with a little help from Emma)

, in curling silver ink.

"You had Emma help you?"

His cheeks color. "Uh . . ."

I show him the tag. He sighs. "That's what I get for not

looking at the box. If we're being honest, yeah, I needed a little help."

I untie the ribbon and open the box. Inside is a silver skate on a dainty chain. I take a close look and notice it's engraved with the words—*In your corner. Always.*

My breath catches. "Drew . . ." I run my thumb over the smooth silver. "This is . . . wow. I don't even know what to say."

He shrugs. "You don't have to say anything, Jingle Blades."

I tilt my head. "Jingle Blades?"

"I've just decided it's the perfect nickname for you because you're joy, strength, grace, and grit all wrapped into one amazing person. Your personality shines so bright, it feels like Christmas."

"Jingle Blades . . . I like it," I say softly. It's a unique name that I doubt anyone else has. It's one that Drew made up for me. Just me. "Can you help me put this on?"

He nods and takes it out of the box. I lift my hair, and he drapes the necklace over my neck. Then I kiss him again.

When I pull back, my hand still in his, and I take a breath. "So . . . are you doing anything tonight?"

He smirks. "Another date? Does it involve more glitter?"

"Close," I say, giggling. "All the athletes here have a different charity event that they're hosting, and tonight is my turn. I'll be skating on a small rink at a Christmas tree farm. I might not be free for the first hour or two, but I was hoping we could hang out afterward."

He laughs under his breath. "Chloe, the farm you're going to . . . it's my parents' place."

My jaw drops. "Wait. Seriously?"

"Yep." His grin deepens. "Sullivan Pines. Right outside town."

A memory tugs at the corner of my mind as soon as I hear the farm's name, from when I got back to our dorm room one year after Thanksgiving break and was given quite the surprise.

I had just opened the door, calling out, "Honey I'm ho—" Then I was smacked in the face by a wall of pine needles. "What on earth?" I yelped, stumbling back. A massive Christmas tree was wedged halfway into the room, blocking the doorway.

"Good timing, Clo! I just got back too. A little help?" Emma's voice floated from somewhere behind the tree.

"I—what is this?"

"A tree," she said matter-of-factly, like I was the one asking dumb questions. "It's too big. I thought it would fit."

I couldn't even see her through the branches. "You brought a full-sized Christmas tree into our dorm room?"

"Yup. Drew helped me drive it down from Colorado. He was heading back to LA anyway with a half-empty truck bed. I figured we might as well use all the space available. So I asked if we could stop by my parents' Christmas tree farm and grab one. Why pay for one here when I can get a tree for free?"

"I thought your parents owned a flower shop."

"They do. And a tree farm—Sullivan Pines. It helps pay the bills in winter when flower sales drop."

Emma's head popped out from the tangle of needles. "So? Can you help me trim the back? If we cut off enough branches, I think it'll fit where the mini fridge was."

"Where's the fridge?"

"In my closet."

I rubbed my temples. "Do you have any pruning shears?"

"No, we'll, um . . . have to use scissors."

I blinked slowly. The only scissors we had were the kind that you used in grade school. I doubted they'd cut the tree very well. "I need coffee first," I said, passing Emma my suitcase through the tree branches.

"Would you mind getting me one too? Oh, and a muffin. Chocolate, if they have it. I'll pay."

"Deal."

The memory fades as I look back at Drew, still smiling like he knew I'd piece it all together eventually.

"So it's a yes?" I ask, my voice light.

"It's a date." He winks. "Our first *real* one."

My chest tightens, like I'm being given a hug. I refrain from jumping up and shouting "yes" at the top of my lungs, trying to play it cool. "Awesome."

After Drew and I part ways, I take a quick detour into the gift shop on my way back to my room. It takes me ten minutes to find exactly what I'm looking for—a keychain shaped like a fish tank, complete with a miniature goldfish floating in a plastic bubble.

"This is perfect," I mutter. It's silly, but I can't help it. I saw it, and I immediately thought of him.

My fingers brush the pendant he just gave me. This little keychain doesn't compare to Drew's gift, but I know it'll make him smile. It's only a placeholder until I can come up with something that feels right.

"Do you need a bag, miss?" the cashier asks me.

"Yes, and a pen if you have it."

The cashier nods and hands me the items. Tucking the keychain into the small paper bag I scribble on the tag—

In case you forget how many lives you saved this week. -C

I leave the package at the concierge desk with his name on it. Emma will make sure it gets to him. Hopefully before our date tonight.

Chapter Sixteen

DREW

There's something surreal about hearing a girl you've fallen for admit she has feelings for you too. Especially when that girl happens to be Chloe.

Now that everything's out in the open, I should feel lighter. And in some ways, I do. My chest isn't weighed down by what-ifs anymore. Chloe and I have both told one another how we feel. And now we're on our way to the next step. I just hope I don't screw it up because I *really* like her. More than anything, I want her to be my girlfriend.

But there's still one thing that's distracting me—the aquarium for the charity ball. I run a hand through my hair and glance at the mess spread out across my desk. There are some half-finished sketches, color-coded sticky notes, and a printout of the ballroom layout, all scattered like confetti. As soon as I got home from talking to Chloe, I spent the rest of the afternoon working on it. I've made some decent progress.

I've sourced the fish, and I've got about half the decorations I need being shipped overnight to the resort. I should still be working on it right now. This is the biggest opportunity I've had in a long time. If I get it right, it could turn into a career doing something I love. But then I picture Chloe's gorgeous face, and I remind myself that she's more important than any job. When I worked for Pacific Skyways, I made the mistake of putting work first.

Although my life in LA may have seemed glamorous, I was always lonely. I lived to work when I should've been working to live. Being let go was probably one of the best things to happen to me. It was the wake-up call I needed to get my butt moving and to start living my life to the fullest.

I'll pull an all-nighter working on the tank tonight if I have to, but I'm not about to give up my shot at spending some time with Chloe tonight. After all, this is our first real date. It'll set the tone for our relationship. If I want her to be my girlfriend, I need to pull out all the stops.

Just as I'm debating whether I have time to add another layer of paint to some of the pine trees I've molded before I leave, the basement door creaks open. "I come bearing offerings," Emma announces dramatically, descending the stairs carrying a small paper bag like it's a crown jewel on a velvet pillow.

I eye the bag warily. "Please tell me that's not another candle. This room already smells like a Bath & Body Works."

"Nope. Even better." She drops it onto my desk with a dramatic flourish. "Special delivery from your *girlfriend* for one overly romantic fish nerd."

Hearing her say "girlfriend" sends a stupid grin across my face. "What is it?"

"No idea. I was *this* close to peeking. But I behaved." She pauses. "Mostly."

Curious, I open the bag and pull out a keychain of a goldfish floating inside its tank. There's a note attached, scrawled in Chloe's neat handwriting—

In case you forget how many lives you saved this week. -C.

"This is perfect." I chuckle, shaking the keychain and watching the blue oil or whatever's inside swish from side to side.

Emma watches me and lets out an exaggerated sigh. "You two have officially crossed into Hallmark movie territory."

I remove my house key from my pocket and clip Chloe's gift onto it. "I'm one lucky guy."

Emma leans against the door frame with a groan. "You used to be cool. Now you're talking to novelty keychains."

I glance over. "I was never cool."

"Fair," she says. "But still. You've got it bad."

I don't even pretend to argue. "I really do. Chloe's the perfect girl."

By the time I pull into the parking lot of my parents' Christmas tree farm, the sky's turned a dusky violet, and the first stars are beginning to poke through the clouds. I glance at the bouquet of flowers on the passenger seat. I picked up some white and red tulips from the shop on my way here and wrapped them in brown craft paper. I debated whether bringing them tonight was too much. But then I remembered who they were for.

You don't show up to a date with Chloe without flowers. Not if you're smart. I just hope she still likes tulips. I remember when I found out they were her favorite flower on her graduation day.

"Did you remember to bring the flowers?" Emma had asked right after the ceremony, yanking me aside as she peeled off her cap and gown.

It was about a hundred degrees, and I had no idea how she'd even lasted the duration of her commencement.

"Yes," I said, holding up the wilted bouquet. The petals had already started to brown at the edges. "But I'm not sure they're presentable."

Emma shook her head. "Clo isn't the type of person who cares about how something looks. It's all about the thought. Tulips are her favorite flowers."

I thought it was strange that Chloe's own family wouldn't have a massive bouquet ready to give her. Emma hinted to me that her parents were well off. But just as my sister had predicted, Chloe loved them.

"These are for me?" she said when I gave them to her, blinking in surprise.

"Yeah, they are. Congratulations."

She held the bouquet to her chest. "Thank you. Tulips are my favorite flower."

"Emma told me. Oh, this is for you too." I placed a lei of purple flowers around her neck.

A small tear trickled down Chloe's cheek. "I didn't think . . . I never expected anyone to . . . just thank you."

She hugged me tightly. I stiffened, then relaxed and wrapped my arms around her. She smelled so good. Like nectarines and lemons. "You're welcome. We're proud of you." I didn't know why I added that, but it felt right. Just like how I didn't want to let go of her.

I'd only met Chloe a handful of times, but I'd always thought she was kind, smart, and funny. Emma knew how to pick good friends.

"Chloe!" Emma cut in, bounding over.

I reluctantly released Chloe. She adjusted her cap.

"Did you get lei-ed yet?" Emma asked.

I groaned. My sister was just as bad as I was with the jokes sometimes.

"I did." She smiled brightly and wrapped both of us in a tight hug. "Thank you for these."

"Drew brought the leis! The tulips were my idea."

Chloe released us and gave me a huge smile. Before I could come up with anything witty to say, however, Emma linked her arm through Chloe's elbow and stole her away. "Come on, my parents are ready to take us out to celebrate. And aren't you dying to take off that cap and gown? Actually, we'd better get some pictures together in it first. Shoot. I wish I hadn't returned mine already."

As they walked ahead, I stayed back for a second, watching them laugh, wondering quietly, where was Chloe's family?

I blink back to the present as I step out of the truck. A few of the workers in Santa hats recognize me and wave as I follow the slow-moving crowd past the welcome booth. Christmas music drifts through the speakers lining the trees. The scent of pine and kettle corn fills the air. Strings of lights crisscross overhead, stretching across the farm's main path.

From the wreath-covered booths selling cider and cocoa to the hand-painted signs pointing the way to the carriage rides, tree-cutting trails, and Santa meet-and-greet.

Dad outdid himself this year. I should've asked him for

a job here instead of at the flower shop. At least it would've been more interesting than being the delivery guy.

"Wow, Mom, look! Santa's reindeer!" a kid shouts, darting toward the petting zoo.

I glance over and smile. The reindeer are a new addition this year, on loan from one of my dad's buddies up in the Rockies. The usual cast of characters—our resident goats, chickens, sheep, and an obnoxiously stubborn old donkey named Waffles—are already drawing a crowd. But none of that holds my attention for long.

My gaze drifts toward the far end of the clearing, to the temporary rink Dad and his crew built for the season. And that's when I see Chloe. My breath catches. She stands at the center of the ice in a red dress that sparkles under the lights like thousands of tiny little stars. Her hair's pulled back into a sleek ponytail and her cheeks are flushed a rosy pink from the cold.

The opening notes of "Jingle Bell Rock" start to play over the speakers. She jumps, spins with her arms lifted gracefully overhead, and stretches her leg behind her high into the air. I've watched plenty of clips of her skating, but seeing her in person, I realize it didn't do her talent justice. And to think, she could be *my* girlfriend if my luck holds.

When she finishes the final spin and strikes her ending pose, the crowd around the rink claps and cheers, and I shove two fingers in my mouth to let out the loudest whistle I can manage. She catches sight of me. Our eyes lock, and I lift the bouquet I've been clutching for the last ten minutes, suddenly aware of how sweaty my palms are from holding them. She shoots me a smile that I know is meant only for me. A shiver of delight travels up my spine.

"Let's hear it again one more time for Chloe Reynolds, your reigning US national figure skating champion!" Mr.

Mynt calls out. Tonight, he's in a red velvet tuxedo, green tie, and Santa hat.

The crowd erupts again, and Chloe bows with effortless grace before gliding toward the side of the rink

Mr. Mynt hands her a microphone. "Thank you to all of you for coming out," she says, her voice warm and easy. "I'm so pleased to say that all proceeds from tonight will support the Winterbrook community. So don't be shy about treating yourselves to a good time!"

The crowd laughs.

Mr. Mynt takes back the mic. "If you'd like to meet Chloe, she'll be signing autographs and taking photos near Santa's workshop."

She flashes one last smile to the crowd, but when her gaze flicks back to me, it lingers. And suddenly, all the nerves I've had about tonight fade away.

I hover near the edge of the crowd as people begin to shuffle toward the photo booth beside Santa's workshop. The whole thing is decked out with garlands, faux snow, and two oversized candy canes that frame the entryway to make the perfect backdrop for a Photogram picture. Chloe's name is stenciled across the banner hanging above the booth, along with a sparkly gold "National Champion" sign.

I join the line, which winds past a booth selling gingerbread cookies and another with hand-painted ornaments. Kids giggle as they clutch signed postcards, beaming as they pose beside Chloe. It's a side of her I haven't seen up close before. This Chloe isn't the shy, quietly driven girl I've gotten to know. She's a polished pro.

I watch as she takes the time to chat with each person as if they're the only ones who matter, making them feel special. She's making me fall even harder for her.

Finally, it's my turn.

"Hey there, stranger," she says, stepping out from behind the booth as a volunteer waves the next group of fans forward.

"I was hoping to meet the famous Jingle Blades," I say, holding out the now slightly crumpled bouquet. "But I'll settle for you."

She laughs. "You brought me flowers?"

"You deserve them."

"I love them." She takes the bouquet with both hands and tucks it close to her chest, inhaling the scent.

I didn't think tulips actually had one, but I could be wrong. I don't go around actively smelling flowers since most of them make my eyes water and my throat burn.

"They remind me of the ones you gave me back in Fresno. I still have those, you know," she says softly.

My heart stumbles. "You kept them?"

She nods, looking up at me through dark lashes. "Pressed them in one of my old journals." She tilts her head slightly, her gaze lingering on my face. "Are you okay? You look like you haven't slept."

I shrug, offering a sheepish smile. "It's been a long day."

But before I can say anything else, a volunteer approaches with an apologetic smile. "Sorry, but we've still got a few more guests in line," she says, nodding toward the cluster of families behind me. "We need to keep things moving."

Chloe sighs and smiles at me, regret flickering across her face. "Duty calls."

"I'll wait," I say, stepping aside. "Take your time."

She squeezes my hand before she turns back to the booth. I find a spot by the cocoa stand and continue to watch her work her magic. Every now and then, I catch a few glances she sneaks in my direction, like she's checking to make sure I'm still there. *Don't worry, Chloe, I'm not going anywhere.*

Chapter Seventeen

CHLOE

I try to stay focused on the long line of fans. Some are shy. Some are bouncing with excitement. But every time I look up, I can't help but glance over to Drew, who's standing near the hot chocolate booth with his hands in his coat pockets.

He has the same soft smile on his face he wore when he handed me the flowers. My body wants to melt like the whipped cream on top of a peppermint mocha. I can't believe he was so thoughtful *and* remembered I like tulips.

But I also notice the faint shadows under his eyes and the way he leans slightly against the booth, like he's trying not to look tired. I make a mental note to keep things low-key tonight. He's doing all of this for me.

I sign another postcard and pose for a photo with a little boy who tells me I "jump better than a dolphin." I thank him and hand him a candy cane before turning back to the next guest. But the whole time, my heart is ticking down the minutes until I can spend time with Drew.

When the last signature is scribbled and the final selfie snapped, I step away and finally let out a slow breath. He's still waiting. For me. Me. I can't believe this is really happening!

I throw a thick parka over my dress, then head straight for him. I'm not about to waste the extra time to change. "Sorry that took so long."

"Chloe, don't apologize. You were doing your job." He grins and hands me a fresh cup of cocoa. This one's topped with twice the peppermint bark, two marshmallows, and a cinnamon stick that doubles as a stirrer.

My heart flips. "You really are trying to win best date of the season, huh?"

He lifts a shoulder. "Just playing to my strengths." Then he hesitates. "Actually . . . I was wondering if you'd help me with something."

"Sure," I say, sipping the cocoa. It's perfect. "What's up?"

"I need to pick out a Christmas tree."

"It's December twenty-first and you're only picking one out now?"

He gives me a crooked smile. "Let's just say I want this one to be special."

I arch my eyebrow. "Is this a 'you grew up doing this every Christmas' kind of tradition? Or more of a 'you forgot and are now scrambling' kind of thing?"

He laughs. "It's a little of both. We always helped pick out the family tree when I was a kid. But the last few years? Life got in the way. This year, I want to make it count."

I file the information away for the future. Another piece of him I hadn't seen before. "Where are you going to put it?"

He zips his mouth closed and tosses away the key.

I cover my mouth with my hand and giggle. "Okay, I get it. Lead the way."

"Do you need to change first? I don't want you to freeze."

"No." I shake my head. "I'm fine. These have a fleece lining," I say pointing to my tights. "And the parka feels like a weighted blanket."

"Wow, that's smart. I didn't know it was something skaters wore."

"We don't normally." I giggle. "It was just for tonight since I knew it'd be cold out here."

We fall into step, following the snow-dusted path past the glowing booths. The sounds of laughter fade the farther we walk, replaced by the soft hush of falling snow and the crunch of our boots.

The pine trees grow taller and thicker the deeper we go. Drew slows down near a quieter patch at the edge of the farm, where it's just the two of us and rows of trees stretching in every direction.

He glances around, then says lightly, "I think the one I'm looking for is out this way."

I raise an eyebrow. "And you know this how?"

He just grins. "Call it intuition."

"You sound like Emma."

He's got one hand stuffed in his coat pocket; the other brushes against mine every few steps. He doesn't take it, but I'm not about to waste an opportunity, so I make the move. His hand is warm, and a little larger than my own.

"Are you really not going to tell me what this tree is for? Will I have to keep guessing until spring?"

He chuckles, sending a cloud of breath into the cold air. "I promise, you'll find out soon enough."

I roll my eyes. Trying to extract secrets from the Sullivan siblings is like taking a bite of toffee. It's so darn hard!

He stops in front of a tree and tilts his head, studying it. "What do you think? Too short?"

Before us is a perfectly cone-shaped tree, close to six feet tall. Its branches are dusted with a light coating of snow, as if someone sifted powdered sugar over them just for effect. I cross my arms and pretend to consider it, even though I have no idea what he's looking for. "Depends. Are you trying to make a statement or play it cool?"

He laughs. "Let's say it's somewhere in between."

"Then this is it," I say, stepping back to admire it from a few different angles.

He gives me a playful side-eye. "I'll add a tag to it so one of the guys can cut it down."

I nod and exhale slowly. Spending time with Drew is everything I've ever wanted, but there's something beginning to gnaw at me from the inside out. A quiet anxiety that's been building since the moment our kiss ended, and the real world started creeping back in. "Drew . . . what happens when I return home to Sequoia Valley?"

He doesn't answer right away, continuing to stare at the tree. The wind picks up, rustling the pine branches overhead. He slides his hands into his pockets, then turns to face me.

"We figure it out," he says simply. "We call, we text, we do cheesy video chats where I try and make you laugh. And when I get some time off, I come to visit you. That is if you want me there."

I search his face. "You'd really do that?"

"For you? I'd risk flying through a blizzard with a sleigh and eight reindeer."

I laugh. "Even Donner? He's the temperamental one."

"I'll bring backup carrots."

He reaches for my hand and laces our fingers together.

"Look, I don't know how all of this will work out. But I know how I feel about you. And I'm not about to let a little thing like geography get in the way now that we've finally decided to try being together. Especially when I should've said something a few years ago."

I nod. My fingers tighten around his. "You're not the only one who should've said something sooner."

He blinks in surprise.

"I used to overthink everything. And I still do. Especially when it comes to people I care about. It's easier to stay quiet than risk messing things up." I take a deep breath. "But you make it easy to talk. This. Us. It's all new for me."

His gaze softens, and I feel it again—a flutter in my chest that tells me this isn't just a crush anymore.

"Okay," he says. "We'll figure it out. Together." His grin spreads slowly, melting whatever lingering doubt was lodged in my chest. "Come on, Jingle Blades. I've got one more surprise for you."

I raise an eyebrow. "Does it involve glitter?"

"Thankfully, no." He leads me down another path, away from the hustle and bustle of the booths. I hear it before I see it—the steady clop of horse hooves, the jingle of harness bells, and the soft creak of wooden wheels rolling over fresh snow.

Just ahead, a horse-drawn carriage waits for us, draped in garlands and twinkling with delicate white lights. Red plaid cushions line the bench seats, and a thick wool blanket is already folded neatly across one side

I stop in my tracks. "Oh Drew, do we get our own carriage?"

"Uh-huh." He grins and winks. "It's one of the perks of being part of the family that runs the place. We can make *anything* happen."

A worker gives us a cheerful wave as he opens the little door. Drew offers me his hand and helps me step into the carriage. The seat cushions are soft and warm. He climbs in beside me and settles the blanket over both our laps as the horses move forward with a gentle nudge from the driver.

The wheels creak, the bells chime, and the world slows to a hush around us. The lights from the farm's main barn twinkle in the distance. We pass rows of evergreens dusted with white and strung with lights.

"I used to think this place was kind of corny," Drew admits, tucking one arm around my shoulders. "But sitting here with you? I think I was wrong. Being with you here is my idea of a perfect night."

"That line was corny, but you know what? This is my idea of a perfect night too." I lean into him, resting my head on his shoulder as the cold melts into the warmth between us.

Chapter Eighteen

DREW

Sleep is for the weak. Or at least that's what I keep telling myself. I've been running on nothing but caffeine fumes and stubbornness since Chloe and I parted ways after our date last night. My eyes are twitching, and I'm pretty sure the dull ache behind my temples might be a permanent fixture by now. But it'll all be worth it.

I kneel back, wincing at the sharp stab of protest from my knees, and survey the tank setup. My fingertips are raw from meticulously spreading the snow-white substrate and carefully arranging miniature lava-rock hills. Even blinking feels like sandpaper against my eyelids, but the foundation looks good.

If the centerpiece arrives on time—which, fingers crossed, it will—I'll finally get to start assembling the miniature model of Mynt Peak Resort. I called about a hundred stores before I finally found a company that could 3-D print the piece within twenty-four hours. Thank goodness I have an unlimited budget because it was *not* cheap. If my luck holds, it'll be just what I need to impress Mr. Mynt enough to trust me with designing more tanks for the resort.

But just in case things don't go as planned, my backup decorations sit neatly lined up at a makeshift workstation in the corner. Miniature wreaths, tiny wrapped presents, and white-dusted fake trees fill every inch of the table. My hands ache. I spent hours painting them. Failure isn't an option. Not now. Not when I'm this close to the finish line.

Rubbing my gritty eyes, I glance at my clipboard lying near the filter system. The notes I scribbled sometime around three a.m. are nearly illegible. At least the water is clear, the lights are installed, and the base is solid. I check my watch. There's less than twenty-four hours left. Nothing like cutting it close.

I groan softly, stretching the sore muscles in my back. Chloe's got a packed schedule today. As much as I'd love to see her, I desperately need uninterrupted time. Well, mostly uninterrupted. My shoulders slump. I still have that stack of floral deliveries waiting for me at the shop. Another sigh slips out. Oh well. Despite all the exhaustion, last night was worth it.

Just thinking of Chloe nestled beside me in the carriage, bundled beneath blankets and smiling up at the snowy trees, warms me better than any espresso shot. I lean forward, resting my forehead against the cool glass of the tank. Chloe's smile floats behind my eyelids.

"Hey, Sleeping Beauty." Emma's voice is louder than normal as it echoes through the empty ballroom.

I open my eyes. "My hero." Once again, my sister is saving the day. She's carrying a tray with two oversized coffees and a bag that promises breakfast pastries.

"Whoa. You look like you've been dragged behind Santa's sleigh all night."

"Thanks. That's exactly what every guy wants to hear." I rub my face again and glance down at myself. Paint-spattered jeans, rumpled hoodie, and what I'm guessing are raccoon eyes. "You should see the other guy."

Emma snorts, handing me one of the coffees.

"What are you even doing here? Don't you have guests to charm at the front desk or something?"

"It's my break." She shrugs, eyeing the partially concealed tank setup. "Speaking of charming, what exactly are you doing in here? Did Santa's workshop explode?"

"It's a secret project," I say with mock seriousness. "Highly classified."

She arches an eyebrow. "So classified that it looks like a kindergarten craft hour threw up all over it?"

I chuckle despite myself. "It's going to look amazing when it's finished, okay? Trust the process."

She squints at me suspiciously. "Does this secret have anything to do with the mysterious tree you and Chloe spent forever picking out?"

"Maybe. How do you know about it?"

"She told me." Emma tilts her head, smirking. "Is it for the ball?"

"Maybe."

"Fine. Be cryptic." She rolls her eyes, clearly disappointed. "But you better at least let me help decorate it. You might have great taste in women, but you have terrible taste in ornaments."

"Wow, thanks for the vote of confidence." I take a long gulp of coffee. "Did you really come here to just insult my decorating skills?"

She grins wickedly. "Obviously. It's my sisterly duty to keep your ego in check. And keep you caffeinated." She steals a quick glance around the ballroom again. "Seriously, though, Drew. Whatever you're working on here, I'm sure it's gonna blow everyone away. Especially Chloe."

Warmth spreads through my chest at her words. "I hope so."

Emma squeezes my arm briefly, her teasing replaced with genuine support. "Get some rest soon, okay? Or at least take a nap."

With a last laugh, she heads toward the door, waving goodbye as she leaves me alone once more with my caffeine and the aquarium.

I take a deep breath, reenergized by the coffee, and walk over to the doors leading to the snowy terrace outside the ballroom. Draped in a tarp in the corner is the tree. It's exactly where I'll need it when it's time for the ball tomorrow night. I can't wait to surprise Chloe with the special decorations I've picked out.

Hours later, I've somehow managed to cross every floral delivery off the list, placed about seventy-five percent of the decorations, and still remember my own name. Barely.

Every part of me aches, but it's nearly done. I wipe my hands clean on a rag, stepping back to survey the setup one last time. The miniature replica of the resort arrived about an hour ago. It turned out even better than I imagined.

Once the fish arrive tomorrow morning, I'll acclimate them and then add them to the tank for the event. Eventually, this will be their permanent home, but until it can be cycled, they'll live temporarily in the tank in my parents' basement.

As I pick up my phone to snap a picture, I notice a message. My heart speeds up when I see Chloe's name flash across the screen.

> Chloe: Just finished the last lesson of the day. There's a sleigh-ride event happening tonight. Are you interested in joining me?

I rub my palm across my jaw, torn. Everything in me wants to say yes, but my body feels like it might give out if I so much as stand too quickly. Still, it's Chloe. Saying no feels impossible.

I hesitate. My fingers hover over the screen.

> Drew: *Thumbs-up emoji.* That sounds great. What time?

If I can nap for two hours, that should be *just* enough to bring me out of zombie mode.

> Chloe: Seven? Unless you want to grab dinner together, then six?

I wince, checking the time. It's five-fifteen already. I glance down at my clothes. They're rumpled and covered in paint and grime. I'll at least need a shower and to change before I can go anywhere near Chloe.

> Drew: I need a little time to wrap up what I'm working on. So seven?

> Chloe: Deal!

My chest tightens with anticipation. I quickly snap the photo of my tank, then open my messages to Emma. Hopefully I can catch her before she leaves the resort.

> Drew: Can I bum a ride off you to the 'rents house?

She replies instantly.

> Emma: It'll cost you.

Drew: I'll pay whatever you want.

> Emma: You must be desperate.

Drew: I am. Just name your price.

Three dots blink as Emma types.

> Emma: I need to think about it. I'll get back to you. In the meantime, meet me at the car. I'm clocking out now.

Drew: Just need to put a few boxes away. See you there.

I pocket the phone, relieved, and turn to the scattered boxes still cluttering the floor. All I need is a quick cleanup and a power nap. Then I'll meet Chloe. I can do it. I hope.

Chapter Nineteen

CHLOE

I smooth down the dark-blue satin of my dress one final time, then slip my gray coat over it, tying the belt tightly around my waist. This outfit was a splurge and supposed to be for the ball tomorrow night, but I wanted to look special for Drew. I hope he doesn't mind that I'll be wearing it twice.

Outside the resort windows, snow falls softly, frosting the trees in a fresh white blanket. My stomach tightens with excitement. After last night's carriage ride, I've barely been able to stop replaying every moment in my head. I can still feel Drew's body pressed next to mine and remember how natural it felt to rest my head on his shoulder.

Glancing at the clock, I realize it's already seven-fifteen. Grabbing my purse, I hurry down to the lobby. I hope he's not mad that I'm running late. Drew's usually right on time, if not early.

The elevator doors open into the bustling lobby, but Drew's nowhere in sight. Strange. But it is snowing. Maybe he just got caught up. Trying not to worry, I wander closer to the grand piano, nodding politely as the resort's pianist launches into a soft rendition of "White Christmas."

A half hour slips away. By seven forty-five, anxiety begins to take hold. I check my phone. There's no missed calls or texts.

This isn't just nerves. This is fear and history repeating itself. Nick didn't text either. He vanished the day I thought he'd be there, and the silence was louder than any apology could have been.

And now? I know Drew isn't Nick. But silence feels the same, no matter who it comes from.

I shoot Drew a quick message:

> Chloe: Hey. Just checking in. I'm in the lobby. Are you nearby?

A minute stretches into ten, then fifteen, without a response. My heart sinks. Did he change his mind? Was last night too much, too soon?

I try calling, but it rings straight to voicemail. My heart sinks further.

Swallowing down rising panic, I pull up my messages with Emma.

> Chloe: Sorry to bug you, Em, but you haven't been in touch with Drew lately, have you?

My phone screen lights up with Emma's name a minute later.

"Hey, Clo. What's up? Is something wrong?"

"Emma." I move away from the pianist, trying to keep my voice steady. "Drew was supposed to meet me for the sleigh ride at seven, but he hasn't shown and he's not answering my messages."

"Wait, really? Weird. We got home an hour ago, and he said he was gonna shower and head right back out. Hang on." I hear footsteps and the sound of a door creaking open. "Drew? Are you decent?" Emma's voice fades briefly, muffled, before she returns to the phone. "Chloe?"

"Still here."

"He's asleep. Like, deep asleep. I shouted his name, and he didn't even flinch. I knew he was exhausted, but wow."

"Oh." My chest tightens painfully. Disappointment flows through me. Why didn't he just tell me he was too tired? "I guess that explains it."

Emma sighs sympathetically. "Drew's so stubborn. He never knows his own limits. That dumb fish tank isn't worth all the stress."

I pause, confused. "Fish tank?"

She hesitates, then continues quickly, sounding slightly guilty. "Yeah, it's this aquarium thing he's been obsessively working on for Mr. Mynt for tomorrow's ball. Honestly, it's been driving him crazy."

I let out a slow breath, my hurt softening into reluctant understanding. He's been pushing himself way too hard. Typical Drew, always giving a hundred percent.

"Do you want me to wake him?" Emma asks quietly. "I don't mind."

"No," I reply. "If he's that exhausted, let him sleep."

"I'm sorry, Chloe. I know he really wanted to be with you tonight."

I bite my lip, glancing wistfully toward the guests headed to the sleigh ride. "I know. Hey, since I'm free tonight, do you want to meet up?"

"Duh. You know me. I'm always down for some quality girl time. Give me twenty minutes. And for what it's worth, I promise to make sure Drew makes this up to you."

I hang up, but I don't move. The music drifts around me, cheerful and bright, but it only seems to highlight the hollow ache in my chest. This was supposed to be our night. I wore this dress, curled my hair, and did my makeup just for him.

I glance toward the sleighs lining up outside, horses snorting gently in the cold. Couples bundle closer together, laughter echoing like bells. I want to be angry, but I get it. He has other things to worry about besides me.

Slowly, I pull out my phone and type out a message to Drew.

> Chloe: Heard from Emma you're asleep.
> Get some rest. We'll talk tomorrow.

I hit Send, then slide the phone back into my purse. At least I'll get to see Emma and tonight won't be a total wipeout.

Chapter Twenty

DREW

I wake up in a panic as I roll over. My phone screen is dead, and reality crashes into me harder than a slapshot to the chest.

"No, no, no . . ." Scrambling upright, I run my fingers through my hair. The room spins briefly before I manage to steady myself. I scramble to find my charger and plug it in. It takes a minute or two before my phone lights up. It's ten a.m. and there's a message from Chloe.

Crap. She's going to think I don't care about her! That I ghosted her. When I started decorating our tree last night, I knew my battery was low. I knew it needed charging, but I got distracted. What is she going to think about me?

> Chloe: Heard from Emma you're asleep.
> Get some rest. We'll talk tomorrow.

Guilt twists sharply in my gut, like finding a lump of coal in your stocking on Christmas Day. How could I have fallen asleep? I was supposed to meet her last night. She must've thought I completely blew her off. I bet she's furious, hurt, disappointed, or all three.

I send her a quick text.

> Drew: I'm so, so, so, so sorry. My phone
> died and I overslept. Please forgive me.
> Call me when you get this.

Dragging myself out of bed, I rush through a quick shower, barely remembering to grab clean clothes. What if she doesn't forgive me? What if I've ruined everything?

By the time I reach the ballroom, the late-morning light peeks through the windows, illuminating the tank waiting patiently in the center. At least that looks perfect; it's ready for the fish that are due any minute now.

A door opens behind me, startling me. I spin around to find Emma standing there, arms crossed, eyebrow arched. "Good morning, dunderhead," she says dryly.

I groan, rubbing my face. "How mad is Chloe?"

She sighs. "Honestly? She's disappointed, but fine. She understands you were exhausted. You're lucky she's so patient and forgiving." Emma steps closer to me, her arms crossed. "I hope you know she was *really* looking forward to seeing you, Drew."

My guilt doubles. "I messed this up big time, didn't I?"

"You did. You owe her," Emma confirms, a playful smirk tugging at her lips. "And actually, I just had a thought. I'm cashing in that favor you owe me from yesterday's ride home."

I raise an eyebrow warily. "What favor?"

"The one you promised me."

"I don't remember promising you any favors, but I also don't remember a lot of yesterday afternoon."

"I have a text from you as proof." She grins mischievously and starts to reach for her phone.

"I trust you. What do you want?" I say tiredly, not in the mood for any games.

"With all that's going on, I doubt my girl Chloe ever got around to asking you to be her date to the ball tonight. So your payment is simple—pick her up and make tonight perfect."

I sigh in relief and smile widely. "That's a price I'm more than happy to pay."

Emma gives me a firm nod. "Good. Make sure you wear a suit and a dark-blue tie, so you'll match her. I'm pretty sure she'll be wearing dark-blue."

"Okay. I think I have a blue tie."

"You do. I saw it when I was putting your clothes back in the closet."

My gaze slides toward the corner of the ballroom, where our tree from the farm sits. "If you have a few minutes, I could use some help."

"With?"

"Finishing the tree. I have the rest of the ornaments ready to go."

Emma rubs her hands together. "Show me where and I'll do it on my lunch break."

I point to a box sitting in the corner. She jogs over and peeks inside. "Oh, these look good." She takes out one of the glass bulbs I hand-painted with a figure skate and hockey skate on it to represent our skating lesson. "You get some brownie points from me for putting a personal touch on these."

"Thanks."

With any luck, by the end of the night, Chloe will know exactly how much she means to me. And if I'm really lucky, she'll forgive me too.

A small seed of doubt creeps in. But what if she

doesn't? What if last night made her question everything? I can't stop picturing Chloe standing alone in that lobby, watching the clock, waiting for someone who never came.

I run a hand through my hair. I wouldn't blame her if it didn't. She let me in, and I blew it on the second date. I know one silent day shouldn't erase everything we've started to build, but it might've hurt her more than I realized. And the truth is, I've never cared more about something working out than I do now. I just hope I won't mess up again for a long time after this. I'm determined for tonight to be perfect.

<h1 style="text-align:center">Chapter Twenty-One</h1>

CHLOE

The day passes by in a blur. I spend most of the morning giving lessons, then the afternoon at a luncheon with some VIP ticket holders. I don't have a spare moment until three.

When I check my phone, I notice a text from Drew.

> Drew: I'm so, so, so, so sorry. My phone died and I overslept. Please forgive me. Call me when you get this.

Checking the time stamp, I see that it was sent around ten this morning. I hang my head. Why didn't I make an effort to check sooner? I tap his name. There are a couple rings before I'm sent to voicemail.

"Hey, Drew, I'm sorry I'm calling you back so late. It's been a really busy day. I know this is super last minute, but, um, would you like to be my date for the Merry Mynt Ball? It's tonight at seven. I meant to ask you last night, but well . . . it didn't work out. Anyways, if you could let me know either way, that'd be great. I'm free the rest of the afternoon, so call me whenever."

I hang up and wince at my words. I couldn't have sounded any more awkward. Or desperate. I really hope he says yes, but I don't want to count my chickens before they hatch. Been there. Done that.

I've been stood up before. Forgotten before. By Adam. By Nick. Even by my own parents. Each time, it left me swearing I wouldn't risk it again. But I've worked hard to change that—to find better coaches, to rebuild my confidence, to believe I deserve more than being overlooked. And here I am, dialing anyway. Taking the risk because for once, I want to trust that up. I hope and pray this time he proves me right.

Chapter Twenty-Two

CHLOE

As I enter the ballroom where the Merry Mynt Ball is being held tonight, my breath catches. There are dozens of shimmering lights suspended from the ceiling. Round tables with gold and silver tablecloths are scattered throughout the room. I approach the nearest one. It has a snow globe as its centerpiece, surrounded by a ring of flickering tealight candles.

At the far end of the room, a live band plays jazzy renditions of holiday classics from an elevated stage above the dance floor. I breathe in the signature Mynt Peak mulled wine scent and glance at the trees tucked into corners and alcoves of the room. There are at least half a dozen. Their branches are strung with fairy lights and velvet ribbons. None of them are the one Drew and I picked out together, but I still find myself looking for it anyway.

I should be swept away by it all. But there's a dull ache pressing behind my ribs. I never heard back from Drew. I have no idea if he got my message, or if he's even coming tonight. I'm angry with him. There's no excuse to ghost me. I obviously don't mean that much to him after all.

When I talked to Emma, she was confident he'd be here. But she wouldn't tell me how she knew. The best she could do was a vague, "Trust me." But now, standing here in my dark-blue dress, watching couples sway beneath the soft glow of the icicle chandelier, the silence feels heavier than ever.

I make my way to the refreshment table and pour myself a cup of hot cider. The steam curls around my face as I take a sip and let the spices warm my insides. Up until now, I've been enjoying myself this week. It was magical.

But I can't help but wish I'd never crossed paths with Drew in the first place if this was the ending I was going to get. Then I would've at least been able to enjoy the ball. I take another sip of cider. I wish Emma wasn't working. She'd be the perfect wingman and partner in crime right about now.

I sigh and look for one of the other athletes I've made friends with. At least that way I won't feel so alone. My gaze sweeps the room. That's when the bright giant aquarium catches my eye near the dessert station.

I stare at it, and suddenly I'm back in the hotel hallway with a dripping-wet Drew. He's got that dark-green algae clinging to his shirt and looks like he'd just lost a fight with a fish. I remember the embarrassment. How certain I was that he'd be furious after I'd crashed into him.

But he wasn't.

It's funny—that one moment unraveled years of distance between us and turned into something more. Was it really only four days ago? It feels like we crammed an entire season into a single snow-dusted week.

I take another sip of cider, then cross the room for a closer look. The aquarium truly looks like something out of a storybook. There's a snowy mountain range rising in the background, complete with frosted peaks and a tiny ski lift inching up the slope. A forest of evergreens, each no taller than a matchstick, frames a cozy lodge built from stacked stone and faux wood, twinkling with lights.

My eyes find the small ice rink, its surface shimmering under tiny overhead lights. A figure is in mid-glide across it in a red dress. I lean in. Huh. It almost looks like me. The dress looks a lot like the one I wore at the Christmas tree event. My heart begins to beat faster. Emma mentioned something about a fish tank and the ball. Is this the one Drew was working on?

A nearby guest murmurs to her partner, "Can you believe one of the floral assistants designed this? Mr. Mynt said he's a local guy. I wonder if he'd do one for my house."

"Drew *did* design this," I whisper.

"I did," a voice says from behind me.

My breath catches. I turn, and there he is. Drew is dressed in a perfectly tailored gray suit, a crisp white shirt, and a silk blue tie that perfectly matches my dress. He stops just a few steps from me, looking slightly winded. His hair is a little mussed, like he got ready in a rush.

"I'm sorry a million times over," he says quickly. "For falling asleep last night. For not calling you back. For making you wonder if I was even going to show." He takes a step closer. "I should've checked my phone earlier. I thought about it at least a dozen times today. But it was one thing after another with the tank. First the fish were late. Then the biological filter stopped cycling properly, so I had to do an emergency water change and reset the whole tank filtration setup and—well never mind. It doesn't matter. The point is, I lost track of time. Again. The whole day slipped away before I noticed I'd ghosted you. If you want to kill me, I give you full permission to. That's twice I've screwed up now."

He lowers his chin and stares at the floor. "I hate that I probably made you feel like you weren't important." Then he takes a deep breath and looks directly at me. "My words sound hollow, but I want you to know that you *are* important to me. More than any project. Any job. Sleep. Food. And well . . . anything."

"Drew, it's okay." My throat tightens. "It may take me a while to get over being frustrated and annoyed with you. But I *do* forgive you. I understand that you were working on a tight deadline. And that you didn't mean to ignore me on purpose. But in the future, you need to promise me you'll take breaks and not throw yourself into the deep end working on something to the point of exhaustion. Or at the very least, send me a text."

He takes hold of my hand and squeezes it tightly. "I promise."

For the first time tonight, I smile. Drew didn't disappear because he didn't care. He was absent because he was trying too hard with the tank. That's who he is. He throws his whole heart into whatever he's focused on. And the truth is that I'd rather have a man in my life who cares too much about something than not at all.

"How did you even manage to get dressed? You said you barely made it here."

"Emma brought it from home." His lips twitch into a sheepish smile. "She even had her coworker Robert follow me to the employee locker rooms to make sure I didn't take any detours while I showered, shaved, and dressed."

I blink. "I'm glad she's on it."

"Me too."

I let out a breath, the tension in my shoulders finally easing. "You're late."

"I'll spend the rest of my life making up for it if you'll let me."

"I don't want to hear about it," I say softly, throat thick with emotion. "I want you to show me."

He takes a step closer. "Gladly." He lifts his hand to cup my cheek, his thumb brushing just beneath my eye. My breath catches. "You're so beautiful, Chloe. My own Christmas fantasy."

And then he kisses me. His lips are warm and sure. I lean into him. My hand drifts up and rests lightly against his chest. Beneath my palm, I can feel the steady rhythm of his heartbeat. It's like sleigh bells in the distance.

His hands slip around my waist, pulling me just a little closer. He smells faintly of peppermint and something else that's clean and light. I'll have to tease him about that later. My fingers curl into the lapels of his jacket as I rise up onto the tips of my toes. The music fades, the chatter disappears, and all I can hear is the sound of our breathing. It's just the two of us.

When we finally break apart, we're both breathless. Drew glances past me, toward the edge of the ballroom. "Come here. There's something else I want to show you."

We slip outside onto the ballroom terrace just as Mr. Mynt steps onto the stage to announce the start of a dancing competition called the Peppermynt Twist Showdown. The air is crisp and still, the kind of cold that makes everything feel quiet and magical. Snowflakes drift lazily from the sky, catching in my hair and on Drew's jacket. And then I see it. Our tree.

Twinkle lights spiral up from the base to the top, glowing soft gold. Glass ornaments catch the light. There's one with snow-covered mountains, one with a horse and carriage, and even a fish ornament nestled near the center.

Strung along the lower branches is a garland made of white ribbon and silver paper stars. I lean closer and realize that each star has something handwritten on it. Tiny words. Little phrases. *First cocoa. Carriage ride. Accidental fish spill.* It's the story of this week told on the tree.

"Merry Christmas, Chloe," Drew says softly.

I glance at him, wide-eyed. "You did all this?"

He nods. "Emma helped me with the finishing touches. The rest was me."

"It's beautiful."

His hand finds mine, his palm warm against the cold. "I know I missed a few things this week. But I didn't want to miss this."

Under the falling snow, we kiss.

At first, it's feather-light, as if he's afraid to cross the line between friendship and something more. My breath catches, and I curl my fingers into his, answering without words that I want this.

He tilts his head, deepening the kiss, and the hesitation melts away. His mouth moves against mine with growing certainty. Each press is more deliberate than the last. His breath hot on my skin. Heat sparks through me, chasing away the cold until the only thing I feel is him.

The world slips out of focus, and suddenly it's as if we're standing inside a snow globe. Flakes swirl around us in a glittering storm, spinning through the glow of the holiday lights until they look like thousands of tiny stars. It's just the two of us. Here. Now. I close my eyes never wanting to forget this moment.

When he finally eases back, it's only an inch. His forehead rests against mine, and his gaze holds mine. In his eyes

I see joy, passion, and the quiet promise that this isn't just a moment. It's the beginning.

Back inside, Drew and I stay long enough to watch the final few couples of the Peppermynt Twist Showdown. The ballroom-style dance-off is one of the few charity events I'm glad I steered clear of. The level of talent the athletes and their professional partners have is unreal. There's no way I could've pulled something like that off in just a few days.

"I can't believe Ledger Bishop pulled off that lift," I whisper to Drew as the well-known Kaisa Halberg dances past us with her professional football partner.

He chuckles. "I didn't know he could be so light on his feet. I've seen him on the football field, but wow."

When they're announced as the winners, the crowd erupts in applause. Kaisa curtsies. Ledger bows.

Drew leans in. "Now *that's* holiday magic."

A few hours later, I tug on Drew's hand as we slip out the back entrance of the ballroom. "Come on." The sky is dark, dotted with thousands of stars as if it's been sprinkled with fairy dust.

He's still in his suit, his tie hanging loose around his neck. "Where are we going?" he asks, but there's a smile tugging at his lips. "Please tell me there's coffee involved."

"No coffee. But I promise it's worth it."

We walk in comfortable silence until the resort's outdoor rink comes into view. The lights are still glowing, casting a soft shimmer across the smooth surface. No one else is around. Just us and the ice.

"Stay here," I say, stopping him with a grin. "I'll be right back."

"What's going on, Jingle Blades?"

"You'll just have to wait and see."

I disappear into the skate rental kiosk, where I had Emma stash my things earlier. It takes me less than three minutes to change into my red skating dress and my skates. As I come out, I hit the play button on the remote to the rink's sound system. The familiar notes of "Santa Baby" play out. I dart onto the center of the ice as Drew turns toward the sound, and I start to skate.

It's far from the best exhibition skate I've ever done. But it's probably one of the most meaningful performances I've ever given. This skate is a gift for Drew. Just him. I thought long and hard about what I could give him to show how much he means to me. And at the end of the day, I decided to show him the story of us through my skating.

Every movement is a page from our story. A donut spin for the night we had cocoa and enjoyed the story hour. A spiral for our meet-cute at the fish tank. A twizzle for that first kiss as a couple. This is my way of saying *I love you*, the way I know best.

When the music fades, I come to a stop in front of him. My chest is heaving from the effort and the nerves. I skate over to the boards. "Merry Christmas," I say.

Drew just stares, stunned, then hops the boards and nearly wipes out on the ice in his dress shoes. He laughs, catches himself, and wraps his arms around me. "You didn't have to give me anything," he murmurs. "But that might be the best gift I've ever gotten."

We kiss. And in that quiet moment, with the snow still falling and the world frozen around us, I know one thing for sure. Christmas has come early. I've received the best gift I could ask for—Drew.

Epilogue

CHLOE

I t's April, and for the first time in months, I've let myself slow down. After a whirlwind competitive skating season filled with long practices, lots of international travel, and a personal-best score at the world championships. I'm finally on vacation, curled up in Colorado with the people I love, about to have pizza.

"Admit it," Emma says, kicking her feet up on her coffee table. "I'm a brilliant matchmaker."

I shake my head and hide my laughter. "Not this again."

"Yes, this again." She chuckles. "I won't give up until either you or Drew admits that the reason you guys ended up together is because of *me.*"

"If you want to get technical, it *was* because of you. He's your brother and—"

"That's *not* what I meant."

"I know." I giggle.

The door opens and Drew enters, balancing two boxes of pizza and a case of black-cherry sparkling water.

"Food's here," he announces. Emma and I both stand

and head over to the table. "I picked up one supreme and one Hawaiian."

"Dibs on the Hawaiian!" Emma grins.

Drew rolls his eyes. "It's all yours. Pineapple on pizza is disgusting." He wrinkles his nose.

"More for me," she says smugly.

"*I* like pineapples on pizza," I tease.

"And you can have some . . . *if* you admit I'm right."

Drew arches his eyebrow. "This again?"

"Yes," I say matter-of-factly. "Fine, Emma, you win. You're the matchmaking queen." She freezes mid-reach for a slice. "If you want that in writing or on video, though, you'll have to wait until after lunch."

"I think you've stunned her into silence," Drew says.

"If I'd have known that would happen, I would've admitted she was right ages ago."

Drew grabs three slices. I peck him on the cheek and help myself to one too.

We've officially been together for four months. And in that time, we've somehow fallen even harder for one another. Although it hasn't been easy being apart for weeks at a time, all that is finally about to change.

Drew's aquarium design business has taken off. My boyfriend is not only the official aquarist for the Mynt Peak Resort, but he's also scored a number of other high-profile clients too, like the Jasper Ridge Resort and Spa and the Scottsdale Sloths Baseball team.

He's just reached the point where he's able to turn it into his full-time job *and* work remotely. We're packing up his life in Winterbrook, and in a few days, we'll be driving out to California. Drew's found an apartment not far from mine in Sequoia Valley, where I'm still living and training.

I thought long and hard about moving to Winterbrook, but after winning my second national championship, placing third at Worlds, and proving to myself that those results weren't flukes, Drew convinced me to stay put. Everything has clicked since I started working with Charlie, Frankie, and Fernando.

In fact, I never thought I'd be in this position, but I'm making a serious run for the Olympics next year. If I make the team, it'll be the icing on the cake to a career I thought was over last year. But if I don't, it's okay too. Because at least I'll be able to retire knowing I'm ending my competitive career on a high note. After that, I have my eye on coaching. I've recently started helping out a bit at the rink, and for the first time, I feel like I have the perfect work-life balance.

Emma eventually snaps out of it and joins us at the table. "Do you need me to run to the store and pick up some more boxes?" she asks, changing subjects.

"No, I think we have enough. Anything that doesn't fit in my truck, I'll either keep here in storage or donate," Drew replies.

Emma nods. "It's going to be weird not having you around."

"Maybe you'll just have to move to California too," I say, only half joking. "The Jasper Ridge Resort and Spa is looking for an experienced concierge to lead the department."

"I'll never say never, but I'm happy where I am right now," she replies.

A part of me deflates. She'd be perfect for that job. After being passed over for the promotion at Mynt Peak, I know the sting's still fresh. But this could be her shot.

"Well, *I'm* not happy about you being here without me. Do you promise not to kill me, Em?" Drew says. We both turn our heads in his direction.

"What did you do?" she deadpans.

"I may have mentioned I have a sister who's a concierge when I met with the hotel owner at my consultation last week. I gave him a rundown of your experience, and he was impressed." Drew wipes his fingers with a napkin, pulls a business card from his wallet, and slides it across the table. "If you change your mind, here's the contact info."

Emma picks up the card. I read over her shoulder. "This isn't HR. This is the owner," she says slowly.

"Like I said. He was impressed," Drew says, casually biting into another slice. "Not to sound overconfident, but it sounded like the job is yours if you want it."

Emma opens and closes her mouth and sets the card down slowly.

"Maybe I just wanted to give you the kind of nudge I wish someone had given me. I'm hoping this cancels out any debts of favors I owe you for a while," Drew adds.

"I . . . I guess it does." She shakes her head and sighs. "But only if I get a job. When we're done here, do you mind if I disappear and work on a cover letter?"

"Do whatever you need to do," he says. "We're in a good spot. All that's left is the stuff in my room. And I'd rather pack that myself."

Emma snorts. "You don't want me going through your underwear drawer."

His cheeks flush. "No."

Watching them go back and forth, I smile to myself. This is what happiness looks like. Not just the big wins, but the quiet moments—shared meals, teasing, and easy laughter.

I didn't grow up with this kind of closeness, but with Drew and Emma, I've found something better. A family I chose. And if Emma takes that job? It'll feel like winning Nationals all over again.

Bonus Content

Thank you for taking the time to read "Jingle Blades." If you enjoyed Chloe and Drew's story, you can unlock a bonus scene and see how they spend their Christmas by joining my newsletter here:

https://tomitabb.com/jingle-blades-bonus-content/

Dear Reader

If you enjoyed this book, please take a moment to leave a review on Amazon, Goodreads, Bookbub, or whatever platform you may have discovered this book on. It helps Tomi connect with readers like you!

Stay connected with Tomi by scanning QR code, or by visiting her official website.

Https://TomiTabb.com

About the Author

Tomi's publishing journey began in 2020 with the release of her debut novel, *Dancing With a Royal*. Although she's always loved writing fictional stories, Tomi's background is in academic writing. She holds an MA degree in History and is currently pursuing her doctorate degree in the same subject.

In her rare free time, Tomi enjoys figure skating and hunting for new pumpkin flavored foods to try. It's one of the many reasons fall is her favorite season.

Tomi is a California native where she resides with her family and one very spoiled cat.

Website: TomiTabb.com

Also by Tomi Tabb

The Unexpected Royals

Dancing With a Royal

Jiving With a Royal

Designing for a Royal

More Than a Passing Shot

Friends of the Unexpected Royals

Designs on Love

Engineering Love

Novellas Related to the Unexpected Royals Series

Pointe Shoes and Sugar Plums

The Skaters of Sequoia Valley

The Rules of the Rink

The Sloth Zone

Caught in a Loop

The Peppermint Playbook Series

Jingle Blades

The Royals of Isola Nostrum

The Great Austen Adventure

For the Love of Dinosaurs

Historical Romance Novellas

The Mysterious Mr. Marcellus

Acknowledgments

Meeting and collaborating with Katie, Larissa, Deb, Michelle, and Taylor over the past year to bring the Peppermint Playbook series to life has been such a fun and rewarding adventure. These ladies are truly amazing and I could not have brought Jingle Blades to life without them.

I have to admit that when Michelle first asked me to join the collab, I was nervous. It was something I'd never done before. When you're an author, you're always on edge when it comes times to put your work out into the universe. But when you're working with other authors, the pressure increases ten fold. Katie, Larissa, Deb, Michelle, and Taylor, however, have made the atmosphere light and playful. And I never felt too much pressure. Writing this book from the beginning has been an absolute joy. And I hope that rings through in the story.

Aside from these ladies, I'd like to thank Gigi Blume for creating such gorgeous covers for the series!

I'd also like to thank Joanne Lui for your keen eyes and top-notch editing skills. You're always more than just an editor, you've become a close friend. I love discussing all things book-related, figure skating, and whatever else randomly seems to pop up with you.

To Charity Chimney, thank you so much for your proofreading prowess. You always help polish my manuscripts to perfection.

To my fellow author Brooke Gilbert, thank you for

always been a close friend and sounding board for all the crazy things life seems to throw our way. I'm so excited for all the adventures for you in the year ahead.

To my family, thank you for always being there with your never-ending love and support. With the latest addition to the family, I would not be able to do this without you.

To my ARC and beta readers, thank you so much for your support. It means the world to me.